KASPAR PRINCE OF CATS

KASPAR PRINCE OF CATS

michael morpurgo

Illustrated by Michael Foreman

HarperCollins *Children's Books*

This edition produced for The Book People Ltd,
Hall Wood Avenue, Haydock, St Helens, WA11 9UL.

First published in hardback in Great Britain by HarperCollins *Children's Books* 2008
HarperCollins *Children's Books* is a division of HarperCollins*Publishers* Ltd
77–85 Fulham Palace Road, Hammersmith, London W6 8JB

The HarperCollins *Children's Books* website address is
www.harpercollinschildrensbooks.co.uk

1

ISBN-13 978-0-00-783045-9

Printed in China

For all the good and kind people at The Savoy
who looked after us so well.

MM.

For my brother Pud,
a North Sea fisher-man and boy.

MF.

Contents

The Coming of Kaspar

Prince Kaspar Kandinsky first came to the Savoy Hotel in a basket. I know because I was the one who carried him in. I carried all the Countess' luggage that morning, and I can tell you, she had an awful lot of it.

But I was a bell-boy so that was my job: to carry luggage, to open doors, to say good

morning to every guest I met, to see to their every
need, from polishing their boots to bringing them
their telegrams. In whatever I did I had to smile at
them very politely, but the smile had to be more
respectful than friendly. And I had to remember all
their names and titles too, which was not at all easy,
because there were always new guests arriving.
Most importantly though, as a bell-boy – which, by
the way, was just about the lowest of the low at the
hotel – I had to do whatever the guests asked me to,
and right away. In fact I was at almost everyone's
beck and call. It was "jump to it, Johnny", or "be
sharp about it, boy", do this "lickedysplit", do that
"jaldi, jaldi". They'd click their fingers at me, and I'd
jump to it lickedysplit, I can tell you, particularly if
Mrs Blaise, the head housekeeper, was on the prowl.

We could always hear her coming, because she
rattled like a skeleton on the move. This was on
account of the huge bunch of keys that hung from

her waist. She had a voice as loud as a trombone when she was angry, and she was often angry. We lived in constant fear of her. Mrs Blaise liked to be called "Madame", but on the servants corridor at the top of the hotel where we all lived – bell-boys, chamber maids, kitchen staff – we all called her Skullface, because she didn't just rattle like a skeleton, she looked a lot like one too. We did our very best to keep out of her way.

To her any misdemeanour, however minor, was a dreadful crime – slouching, untidy hair, dirty fingernails. Yawning on duty was the worst crime of all. And that's just what Skullface had caught me doing that morning just before the Countess arrived. She'd just come up to me in the lobby, hissing menacingly as she passed, "I saw that yawn, young scallywag. And your cap is set too jaunty. You know how I hate a jaunty cap. Fix it. Yawn again, and I'll have your guts for garters."

I was just fixing my cap when I saw the doorman, Mr Freddie, showing the Countess in. Mr Freddie clicked his fingers at me, and that was how moments later I found myself walking through the hotel lobby alongside the Countess, carrying her cat basket, with the cat yowling so loudly that soon everyone was staring at us. This cat did not yowl like other cats, it was more like a wailing lament, almost human in its tremulous tunefulness. The Countess, with me at her side, swept up to the reception desk and announced herself in a heavy foreign accent – a Russian accent, as I was soon to find out. "I am Countess Kandinsky," she said. "You have a suite of rooms for Kaspar and me, I think. There must be river outside my window, and I must have a piano. I sent you a telegram with all my requirements."

The Countess spoke as if she was used to people listening, as if she was used to being obeyed. There were many such people who came in through the doors of the Savoy: the rich, the famous and the infamous, business magnates, lords and ladies, even Prime Ministers and Presidents. I don't mind admitting that I never much cared for their haughtiness and their arrogance. But I learned very soon, that if I hid my feelings well enough behind my smile, if I played my cards right, some of them could give very big tips, particularly the Americans. "Just smile and wag your tail." That's what Mr Freddie told me to do. He'd been working at the Savoy as a doorman for close on twenty years, so he knew a thing or two. It was good advice. However the guests treated me, I learned to smile back and behave like a willing puppy dog.

That first time I met Countess Kandinsky I thought she was just another rich aristocrat. But there was something I admired about her from the start. She didn't just walk to the lift, she sailed there, magnificently, her skirts rustling in her wake, the white ostrich feathers in her hat wafting out behind her, like pennants in a breeze. Everyone – including Skullface, I'm glad to say – was bobbing curtsies or bowing heads as we passed by, and all the time I found myself basking unashamedly in the Countess' aura, in her grace and grandeur.

I felt suddenly centre stage and very important. As a fourteen-year-old bell-boy, abandoned as an infant on the steps of an orphanage in Islington, I had not had many opportunities to feel so important. So by the time we all got into the lift, the Countess and myself and the cat still wailing in its basket, I was feeling cock-a-hoop. I suppose it must have showed.

"Why are you smiling like this?" The Countess frowned at me, ostrich feathers shaking as she spoke.

I could hardly tell her the truth, so I had to think fast. "Because of your cat, Countess," I replied. "She sounds funny."

"Not she. He. And he is not *my* cat," she said. "Kaspar is no one's cat. He is the Prince of cats. He is Prince Kaspar Kandinsky, and a prince belongs to no one, not even to a Countess." She smiled at me then. "I tell you something, I like it when you smile. English people do not smile so often as they should. They do not laugh, they do not cry. This is a great mistake. We Russians, when we want to laugh, we laugh. When we want to cry, we cry. Prince Kaspar is a Russian cat. At this moment he is a very unhappy cat, so he cries. This is natural, I think."

"Why's he so unhappy?" I found myself asking her.

"Because he is angry with me. He likes to stay in my house in Moscow. He does not like to travel. I tell him, 'how can I go to sing in opera in London if we do not travel?' He does not listen. When we travel he always make big fuss, big noise. When I let him out of his basket, he will be happy again. I will show you."

Sure enough, the moment Kaspar climbed out of the basket in the Countess' sitting room, he fell completely silent. He tested the carpet with one paw, and then leaped nimbly out and began at once to explore. That was when I first understood just why the Countess called him a Prince of cats. From his whiskers to his paws he was black all over, jet black, and sleek and shiny and beautiful. And he knew he was beautiful too. He moved like silk, his head held high, his tail swishing as he went.

I was about to leave the room to fetch the rest of

her luggage, when the Countess called me back, as guests often did when they were about to give me a tip. Because of her title, and her ostrich feathers, and all the fine luggage she had arrived with, I was very hopeful by now that the tip might be a generous one. As it turned out she didn't want to give me a tip at all.

"Your name? I wish to know your name," she said, removing her hat with a flourish.

"Johnny Trott, Countess," I told her. She laughed at that, and I didn't mind, because I could tell at once that she was not mocking me.

"That is a very funny name," she said. "But who knows? Maybe for you Kandinsky is a funny name too."

By this time Kaspar had leaped up on to the sofa. He sprang off again almost at once, and went to sharpen his claws, first on the curtain, then on one of the armchairs. After that he went on a tour of the room, behind the desk, in under the piano, up on the window ledge, for all the world like a prince inspecting his new palace, claiming it, before settling down on the armchair by the fireplace, from where he gazed up at us both, blinking his eyes slowly, and then licking himself, purring contentedly as he did so. Clearly the prince approved of his palace.

"He's a very smart looking cat," I said.

"Smart? Smart? Kaspar is not smart, Johnny Trott." The Countess was clearly not at all pleased with my description of her cat. "He is beautiful – the most beautiful cat in all of Russia, in all of England, in all of the whole world. There is no other cat like Prince Kaspar. He is not smart, he is magnificent. You agree, Johnny Trott?"

I nodded hurriedly. I could hardly argue.

"You wish to stroke him?" she asked me.

I crouched down by the chair, reached out my hand tentatively and stroked his purring chest with the back of my finger, but only for a second or two. I sensed that, for the moment, this was all he would allow. "I think maybe he likes you," said the Countess. "With Prince Kaspar, if you are not a friend, you are an enemy. He did not scratch you, so I think you must be a friend."

As I stood up again I noticed she was fixing me with a searching look.

"I wonder, are you a good boy, Johnny Trott? Can I trust you?"

"I think so, Countess," I replied.

"This is not good enough. I have to know for sure."

"Yes," I told her.

"Then I have a very important job for you. During each day I am here in London you will look after Prince Kaspar for me. Tomorrow morning I begin rehearsal at the opera. Covent Garden. *Magic Flute*. Mozart. I am Queen of the Night. You know this opera?"

I shook my head.

"One day you will hear it. Maybe one day I shall sing it for you on the piano, when I practice. Every morning after breakfast I must practice. Prince Kaspar, he is happy when I sing. At home in

Moscow he likes to lie on my piano to listen to me, and he waves his tail, just like now. Look at him. This is how I know he is happy. But when I am at rehearsal I must know that you look after him well, that he is happy. You will do this for me? Feed him for me? Talk to him? Take him for a walk outside, once in the morning, once in the evening? He likes this very much. You will not forget?"

The Countess Kandinsky was not an easy person to say no to. And anyway, the truth is I was flattered to be asked. I did wonder how I would be able to manage it in between my other duties downstairs. But I wondered also whether maybe she'd give me a good tip for it, though I certainly didn't dare say anything about that.

The Countess smiled at me and held out her gloved hand to me for me to take. I hesitated. I had never before shaken hands with a guest. Bell-boys just didn't ever shake hands with guests. But I knew she meant me to, so I did. Her hand was small and the glove very soft.

"You and me and Prince Kaspar, we shall be good friends. I know this. You may leave us now."

So I turned to go.

"Johnny Trott," she said, laughing again. "I am sorry, but you have a very funny name, maybe the funniest name I ever heard. I have decided you are a good boy, Johnny Trott. You know why I think this? You never ask for money. I shall pay you five shillings every week for three months – I am here for three months at the opera. Ah, so now you smile again, Johnny Trott. I like it when you smile. If you had a tail, you would be waving it like Prince Kaspar, I think."

When I brought up her trunks later on and left them in the hallway of her suite, I heard her in the sitting room singing at the piano. I caught a glimpse of Kaspar lying there right in front of her, gazing at her, his tail swishing contentedly. When I left I stayed outside the door for a while just listening. I knew even then as I stood there in the corridor that this was a day I would never forget. But I could never have imagined in my wildest dreams how the arrival of the Countess and the coming of Kaspar would change my life for ever.

Not Johnny Trott at All

I never had a mother, nor a father come to that, nor any brothers or sisters, none that I know of anyway. Not that I have ever felt sorry for myself. The truth is that you don't miss what you've never had. But you do wonder. As a small boy growing up in the orphanage in Islington, I often used to try to imagine who my mother was, what she looked like, how she dressed, how she spoke. For some reason I never much bothered about my father.

I must have been about nine years old, and on the way back from school one day, walking down Tollington Road, when I saw a fine lady passing by in a carriage. The carriage happened to stop right by me. She was dressed all in black and I could see she had been crying. I don't know why, but I smiled at her and she smiled back. At that moment I was sure she was my mother. Then the carriage moved on, and she was gone. For months afterwards I dreamed about her. But as the memory of that moment faded, so did the dream. I had other imaginary mothers of course. They didn't have to be posh or rich, but I certainly didn't want to believe that my mother might be down on her hands and knees scrubbing someone's doorstep, her nose and hands red and raw with the cold. Above all my mother had to be beautiful. She couldn't be too old and she couldn't be too young. She mustn't have children. It was essential to me that I was the only child. And of course, she would have to have fair hair, because I had fair hair.

It was natural then, I suppose, that within a few days I had quite made up my mind that Countess Kandinsky fitted the bill perfectly. She was fair-haired, supremely beautiful and elegant, about the right age to be my mother, and so far as I could tell, childless. So if she was my mother, it followed that I had to be a Russian count or prince – I didn't much mind which. The more I thought about it, the more I liked the idea, and the more I'd daydream about it. I would lie awake in my little attic room up on the servant's corridor, where the roof leaked and the water pipes gurgled and groaned, and I'd dream my dream, knowing of course that it was probably all nonsense, but believing in it just enough for me to be able to enjoy it all the same. Thinking back, I'm sure it was this silly fantasy, as much as my cat-minding duties that made me look forward so much to visiting the Countess' rooms while she was at rehearsals. I went up there at every possible opportunity, as often as I could manage, without my absence in the lobby being noticed. I was always up and down in the lift, carrying luggage, and each time I'd just slip away for a minute or two and check on Kaspar. Mr Freddie noticed of course – he noticed everything.

"What have you been up to, lad?" he asked me once when I came back down.

"Nothing," I told him with a shrug.

"Well, one day," he said, "maybe that nothing will get you into a whole lot of trouble with Skullface. So you'd better watch your step." I knew Mr Freddie wouldn't snitch on me, he wasn't like that.

Usually I'd find Kaspar sitting at the bedroom window, watching the barges steaming by on the

river, or sometimes he'd be curled up asleep in his chair in the sitting room. Either way, he'd hardly deign to give me a second glance until the food was in his bowl, and until he decided he was ready for it. Those first few days, I felt he was treating me in much the same way as most of the guests who came to the Savoy, with a certain cold disdain. I wanted to like him and be liked by him, but he kept his distance. I wanted to stroke him again, but I didn't dare because he made it perfectly clear by the way he looked at me that he didn't want me to. I did dare talk to him though – probably because he couldn't answer me back. I would crouch beside him as he lay in his chair cleaning himself after his meal, and I'd tell him how my name was not Johnny Trott at all, but Count Nicholas Kandinsky – the Tsar of Russia was called Nicholas, I knew that, so I thought the name would do fine for me. I told Kaspar that I was in fact the long lost son of the Countess, that she had come to London to look for me, and that therefore I was to be treated with greater respect, even if he was a Prince, and that anyway there wasn't much difference between a Prince and a Count.

He'd listen for a while to my fantastical ramblings, but he'd soon tire of them, break into a great roaring purr, close his eyes and go to sleep. But then, after only a few days he surprised me by jumping up to sit on my lap after he'd finished his meal. I dared to hope that at last he was beginning to treat me as an equal, that he must have believed my story after all, that we might now be friends. So I stroked him.

Clearly I presumed too much. Kaspar sank his claws into my knee just to remind me who the Prince was, then sprang off my lap and went to the window, where he sat deliberately ignoring me, swishing his tail with quiet satisfaction and watching the barges on the river. I went to stand by him to try to make it up to him.

"And I love you too," I told him. I said it sarcastically, but even as I was saying it, I knew I really did mean it. He was an ungrateful, supercilious creature, and not at all endearing in any way. Yet despite all this I loved him, and I wanted him to love me too. There were moments when, if I'm honest, I relished Kaspar's aristocratic aloofness. Twice a day, during my work breaks, I'd take him out for his walk. We went to the park down by the river, but to get to the park I had to walk Kaspar on his lead from the lift all the way across the lobby to the front door. I swear that Kaspar knew perfectly well that everyone was looking at him, admiring him. He certainly knew how to put on the style, stepping out all high and mighty like the Prince of Cats he was, his tail waving majestically. Did I feel proud! Mr Freddie would doff his top hat to us as we passed by. There was some mockery in the gesture, I knew, but there was something else too. Mr Freddie knew class when he saw it, and Prince Kaspar was class. He left no one

in any doubt about that. Even the dogs in the park knew it. One withering look from Kaspar, and any notions they might have had of the prospect of a good cat-chase withered away instantly. Tails between their legs they would bark at us, but only from a safe distance. Kaspar made it plain that he simply despised them, and then he ignored them.

It was on a bench in the park one spring day, perhaps six weeks or so later, that Kaspar first showed me any real affection. He was sitting up on the park

bench beside me basking in the sunshine, when without even thinking about it I found myself stroking his head. He looked up at me to let me know it was all fine by him, and then he smiled, I promise you he smiled. I felt his head pushing into my hand, felt the purr coming over him. His tail was trembling with pleasure. I know it sounds silly, but at that moment I felt so happy that I was almost purring myself. I looked into his eyes and for the first time I could tell that he liked me, that at last he thought of me as his friend. I felt honoured.

The next morning I met the Countess hurrying through the lobby.

"Ah Johnny Trott," she said, as I opened the front door for her. "I am late for rehearsals. All my life I am late. You will walk with me. I have an important thing I must say to you."

It was raining, so I held the umbrella for her as we crossed the Strand and walked up into Covent

Garden, past the barrel organ with the monkey who turned the handle, and the blind soldier playing his accordion by the fruit stalls. She stopped to pat the coalman's horse, who was standing between the shafts of his cart, hanging his head in the rain, and looking thoroughly miserable and soaked through. The Countess berated the coalman soundly when he came out of the pub, and told him in no uncertain terms that he should put a blanket on the horse in such weather, that in Russia they treated horses properly. The coalman was speechless, too stunned and shamefaced to argue. We walked on.

"I have much to thank you for, Johnny Trott. Prince Kaspar is a very happy cat, happy to be in London. And when Kaspar is happy, I am happy. I sing better when I know Kaspar is happy. This is true. You know how I know he is happy, because he smiled at me this morning. And this he does not do very often, so I know you must look after him very well."

I was about to tell her all about Kaspar smiling at me the day before, but she was in full flow and I didn't dare to interrupt her.

"Because you make us both so happy, Johnny Trott, I wish to invite you to *The Magic Flute*, to the opera at Covent Garden. Tomorrow evening. It is the first night. You will come?"

I was so taken aback I did not even think to thank her. "Me?" I said.

"Why not? You will sit in the best seat. Dress circle. You are a guest of the Queen of the Night."

"I'd really like to, Countess, honest I would," I told her, "but I can't. I'll be working. I don't finish till ten o'clock."

"Don't worry, I fixed this already with the manager at the hotel," she said, with an imperious wave of her hand. "I told him you do not work tomorrow, you have the whole day off."

"But you've got to be smart to go to the opera,

Countess." I said. "I've seen all the grand gentlemen and the ladies. I haven't got the right clothes."

"I'll fix this too, Johnny Trott. You'll see. I'll fix everything."

And so she did. She hired me a suit to wear – the first proper suit I ever put on. I could hardly believe it when I found myself the next day standing in front of her in her sitting-room, all washed and brushed up, while she adjusted my tie and collar.

I remember that I was looking up into her face, and all I wanted to do was to call her "mother", to hug her tight and never let go.

She frowned. "Why do you look at me like this, Johnny Trott?" she said. "I think maybe you have tears in your eyes. I like this. You are a boy with feeling, so you will be a man with big heart. Mozart had a big heart, and he was the greatest man who ever lived. A little mad maybe, but I think you have to be a little mad to be great. I love this man. I tell you something, Johnny Trott. I have no son, no husband. I have only Prince Kaspar and my music. But if I had a husband he would be Mozart, and I say something else: if I have a son, I want him to be like you. This is the truth. Now, Johnny Trott, I take your arm, and you will walk me to Covent Garden. Be proud, Johnny Trott. Walk like Kaspar. Walk tall, like you are a Prince, like you are my son."

This time when Mr Freddie saw me coming and raised his top hat, there was no mockery in it whatsoever, only open-mouthed astonishment. The Savoy lobby fell silent in utter disbelief as we strode through. I felt about ten feet tall, and that's how I continued to feel as we made our way up through Covent Garden market to the Royal Opera House.

*

I should like to be able to say that I remember every moment, every note of my evening at the opera, but I do not. It passed in a blur of wonderment. I do however have a very clear memory of Countess Kandinsky as she made her first entrance as Queen of the Night, the rapturous applause after every aria she sang, and the standing ovation for her at the final curtain. In fact I was so proud of her, so carried away by it all, that I stuck my fingers in my mouth and gave her the loudest, longest whistle I could, ignoring the disapproving looks all around me. I knew full well it was not the thing to do, but I just didn't care. I whistled again and again. I stood and clapped until my hands hurt, till the curtain closed for the last time.

As we walked back to the hotel together later that night I was so laden down with all the flowers she had been given that I could scarcely see in front of me. Kaspar was waiting for us when we got back, yowling around us until I gave him some milk. The Countess went straight to the piano, her hat still on, and began to play softly.

"This I play every night after the opera, before I go to bed. It is a lullaby by Mozart. It is beautiful, no? Prince Kaspar, he likes this very much."

And as if to prove it Kaspar leaped up on to the piano to listen. "Johnny Trott," she went on, still playing. "Do you think they liked how I sang tonight? You must tell me the truth."

"Of course," I told her. "Didn't you hear them?"

"And you, Johnny Trott, do you like how I sing?"

"I never heard anything so wonderful," I said, and I meant it.

She stopped playing and beckoned me over to the piano. She reached up and brushed the hair from my forehead. "You go now, Johnny Trott. It is very late."

The next day Mr Freddie and all the others on the servant's corridor teased me mercilessly. "Who's a Laadeedaa lad then?" They called after me. "Laadeedaa!" Whatever they said, I didn't mind. I was on cloud nine. During our walk in the park that morning, I told Kaspar all about my night at the opera, how everyone there had taken the Countess to their hearts, how she would be the talk of London, that he should be very proud of her. When no one was around I even whistled him a snatch of a tune I had remembered, but this did not seem to impress him at all.

When we came back through the front door half an hour later, I was expecting more of the same banter, more ribbing. I was even looking forward to it. But as I came through the lobby I noticed everyone was behaving very strangely, that they were averting their eyes, obviously not wanting to talk to me. I thought at first they must be angry with me. Mr Freddie came over to me then, and took me gently to one side, to offer me some advice, I thought, something he often did when I'd done something wrong.

"Best get this over with, Johnny," he began. "It's the Countess. She was knocked down an hour or so ago, just outside in the street. An omnibus it was. They say she walked straight out in front of it. Couldn't have seen it coming. We was all very fond of her, you most of all. Almost like a mother she was to you, wasn't she? I'm sorry, Johnny. She was a good lady, a fine lady, and a kind one too."

A Ghost in the Mirror

I cried myself to sleep that night. Mr Freddie was right. The Countess had been like a mother to me – not that I knew what a real mother was like, but she was certainly the mother I had always hoped to find. I had found her, and now she was gone. I had lost as well the first real friend I had ever had, the first person who had ever told me they liked me.

I cannot tell you how grateful I have always been to her for that. In all my life I have never known anyone whose light shone so brightly, so brilliantly and so briefly. The shock of her death stunned everyone. For days afterwards the whole hotel was plunged into a deep sadness.

I hate to have to admit it, but to begin with I was too wrapped up in my own grief to notice Kaspar, nor to think very much about him and what would happen to him, now that the Countess was gone. It took Mr Freddie to jolt me out of my self-pity.

"I've been watching you, Johnny lad," he said to me one evening. "You've been moping about the place all day. You've got to buck yourself up, you have. It won't hardly bring her back, will it? And I'm sure it's not what she would have wanted. You know what she'd have wanted. She'd like for you to go on looking after that cat of hers as well as you can, for as long as you can. And if you're feeling bad, think what that cat must be feeling. So you go up there, Johnny and see to him. The Countess' rooms are bought and paid for another month at least, so I've been told. I reckon it's your job to look after that Kaspar, till someone from the family comes and fetches him away."

So that's what I did, and that's when I began to notice how sad Kaspar had become. That's when I noticed something else too. Every time I went in to be with Kaspar it was as if the Countess was there in the room with me. Sometimes I thought I even smelled her perfume. Sometimes I was sure I heard her humming and singing. More than once, late in the evening, I heard that lullaby playing on the piano. And time and again I thought I caught sight of her in the mirror, but when I turned round she wasn't there. I knew she had been, though. I was certain of it. I wasn't frightened, not exactly. But it troubled me, and made me feel uncomfortable every time I went into her room.

It was obvious to me that Kaspar sensed her presence too. He was not himself at all. He was nervous, restless, anxious. He didn't purr anymore. He'd stopped washing himself, and so far as I could see, he hardly slept. He'd spend hours searching the rooms for the Countess, yowling piteously. He wouldn't eat, he wouldn't drink. He was clearly pining for her. I decided that maybe if I took him out more often, for walks in the park, it might help him. He drank from the puddles then, which was something.

I tried to reassure him all I could. I told him over and over that everything would be all right. Sitting there on our bench one day I promised him faithfully that I'd look after him. But I could see he wasn't listening. More and more he just didn't seem to care. More and more he just didn't seem to want to go on living. I tried feeding him by hand, but he would only sniff at it and turn away. I tried calves liver from the kitchen. I tried best beef, finely chopped. Nothing worked. Kaspar was losing

weight all the time, losing his sleekness. His coat was beginning to stare. He was already the ghost of his former self. There seemed to be nothing I could do to halt his decline. I knew if he went on like this, it could only end one way. Now I would lie awake at night, not grieving for the Countess any more, but trying desperately to think of some way of saving Kaspar's life.

It was during one of these long and sleepless nights that I had an idea. It occurred to me that it was only in the Countess' rooms that I had felt her presence, that I'd caught my fleeting glimpses of her. Maybe it was the same for Kaspar. Maybe that was what was troubling him. If I got him out of those rooms somehow, and away from her, then he might possibly be able to forget her.

I had it in my head that the only thing to do was to bring Kaspar up to my little attic room and look after him there. That way I could also be with him more often. But I knew from the start there would be problems. Sooner or later, as Mr Freddie had said, the Countess' relations would be coming to collect her belongings, and no one knew when that would be. One thing was for sure: they'd be coming for Kaspar too, and they'd expect to find him in her rooms. And if he wasn't there, they'd be bound to ask me where he was. Just about everyone who worked in the hotel knew by now that I had been looking after Kaspar. I couldn't say I was keeping him in my room because we were absolutely forbidden to keep pets in our rooms. The house rules were very strict. No birds in cages, no goldfish, no cats, no dogs, no mice. In fact no friends of any kind were allowed up in the servants' rooms, animal or human. Breaking any of the house rules would lead to instant dismissal – Skullface never showed any mercy. I told Mr Freddie my plans because I knew he'd understand. He said it was far too dangerous to take Kaspar up there, that I'd be out of a job and on the streets just like that if Skullface ever found out about it.

"You don't want to risk everything for a cat,

Johnny," he said. "Not even for Kaspar."

It was good advice. I thought about it long and hard, but in the end I knew I had no choice. I could think of no other way of saving Kaspar. I told everyone on the servants' corridor what I was doing – there was no way I could keep a cat up there in my room and keep it a secret from them. One thing was certain: none of them would snitch on me to Skullface, we all hated her far too much. Besides, they all realised by now just how ill Kaspar was, and they all wanted to help. He'd become quite a favourite.

Late one evening we all crowded into my room where Mary O'Connell, one of the scullery maids, made us all join hands and make a secret pact not to tell a living soul. Mary was an Irish girl from County Galway. She was a powerful character and had a persuasive way with words. She was very religious-minded, and she made us all swear on her bible never to say a word. Luke Tandy, a waiter in the Riverside Restaurant, said he wouldn't swear on the bible because he didn't believe in all that "religious malarkey".

"Well you'd better believe something else then, Luke," Mary told him, wagging her finger at him. "You say a word to a soul, and I'll beat the living daylights out of you, so I will."

All I had to worry about now was Skullface herself. She hardly ever made an appearance on our corridor but we all knew she could come up there any time. We had to keep an eye out for her, but most of all we had to get lucky.

That same night I crept downstairs, let myself into the Countess' room, and carried Kaspar up into his new home in my little attic room. As soon as I got him there I sat him on the bed beside me and gave him a good talking to. "None of your yowling, Kaspar. If Skullface finds you up here, we're done for, me and you both. And you've got to eat. You've got to get better, you hear me?" He didn't yowl, but he didn't eat either. He just lay there curled up on my bed sleeping, and hardly moved. When I left him to go on duty downstairs in the lobby he took very little notice of me. And he took very little notice of me when I came back either. Mary O'Connell tried to feed him, tried to talk him into it, but he wasn't interested. Almost everyone on the corridor had a go. We tried chicken, salmon, even caviar once – anything Mary could filch from the kitchens without being noticed. All of it went uneaten. He wouldn't touch anything, not even his milk.

Just in case the Countess' relatives turned up, I'd put it about everywhere – we all had – that Kaspar had escaped from the Countess' rooms and could not be found. I made a great song and dance about organising a search of the whole hotel, pretended to be beside myself with worry, and I asked everyone to keep an eye out for him. Mr Freddie knew what I was up to of course, but besides Mary and Luke and all the gang on our corridor, no one else did. So now I could only take Kaspar for his walk at night time, when hardly anyone would be about. I'd hurry out the back way, through the tradesmen's entrance, with Kaspar hidden under my coat. While we were out there in the park he seemed to perk up for a while, but it never lasted. Back in my room he would curl up again, and close his eyes. Often I would hear him sighing deeply, almost as if he wished every breath to be his last. It broke my heart to see him like this. I felt so utterly helpless.

Meanwhile the Countess' brother and sister came to take away all her things. They asked after Kaspar, and I told them, as I'd told everyone else, that he'd disappeared. In the Countess' sitting room they stood by the piano for a while and cried on one anothers shoulders. I found myself looking again in the mirror, where I had so often caught a ghostly glimpse of the Countess. I did not see her this time but I felt her presence. I made her a silent promise then and there that I wouldn't let Kaspar die.

As it turned out Kaspar didn't die. He was saved. But I have to say that it had nothing whatsoever to do with me. In the end, Kaspar was saved by happenchance, by pure happy circumstance.

I had seen the Stanton family about in the hotel, but to begin with had paid them little enough attention. They seemed a lot like other rich families that came to stay for a month or two in the hotel. They were American; father, mother, and a little girl.

Both the parents seemed rather stiff and prim and proper, even a bit standoffish, which in my experience was not at all like most of the Americans guests I'd met in the hotel. The little girl was different though. She was about seven or eight, I guessed, and was always in trouble, always being ticked off by her mother. She was for ever wandering off on her own and getting herself lost. As I was soon to learn, getting lost didn't upset her one bit, but it did upset her parents, particularly her mother, whom I'd often see hurrying through the lobby in search of her. It was from her mother, one breakfast time, that I first learned the little girl's name.

"Elizabeth. I'm looking for Elizabeth," she said, rushing up the stairs into the lobby from the Riverside Restaurant. All her usual composure was gone. There was a wild and anxious look about her. "She's run off again. Have you seen her? Have you seen her?"

Fortunately Mr Freddie was nearby. He was always good in these situations. "Don't you worry, Mrs Stanton, we'll find her for you. She hasn't come through the front door, so she's got to be in the hotel somewhere. Young Johnny here will look upstairs. Every floor, Johnny, make sure you search every floor thoroughly. And meanwhile, Mrs Stanton, I'll have a good look around for her down here. We'll have her back with you in a jiffy, lickedysplit. You'll see." He clapped his hands at me. "Off you go, Johnny lad. Jaldi, jaldi. Sharp about it now, there's a good lad."

An hour later I'd searched every floor of the hotel, high and low, and there was still no sign of her. I was about to check downstairs to see if Mr Freddie hadn't already found her, when I wondered if I should check the servants' corridor up in the attic.

I thought it very unlikely she'd be up there, but

Mr Freddie had told me to search every floor. And besides, I remembered my own childhood well enough to know that children like to hide in the most unexpected places. So I climbed the stairs to have a look.

From the far end of the corridor I could already see that the door to my room was open, and I knew at once she must be in there. As I stole along the corridor I could hear her talking inside my room.

"Good cat," she was saying, "nice cat, beautiful cat." I found her kneeling at the foot of my bed. Beside her was Kaspar, eating ravenously from his bowl, wolfing down the liver I had left for him, and purring like a lion.

"Who Gives a Fig, Anyway?"

Elizabeth looked up at me and smiled. "Hello," she said. "My name is Miss Elizabeth Stanton. What's the cat called?"

"Kaspar," I told her.

"Is he yours?"

"Yes," I said. "And this is my room too."

"I knocked and there was no one in," she went

on. "So I thought it would be a good place to hide. I like hiding. Then I saw this cat lying on the bed, and he looked so sad. He's very beautiful, but he's very thin, you know, and he doesn't look at all well. Look at him. He's starving hungry. You should feed Kaspar more often, that's what I think."

"Your mother's been looking for you. She thought you'd got lost," I told her, trying my best to hide my growing irritation. To be honest, I didn't much like being told by some hoity-toity little rich girl that Kaspar needed to eat more. Hadn't I been trying for weeks on end now to get him to do just that? And although I was relieved to see Kaspar eating again, I have to confess I was more than a little upset that this little girl seemed to have succeeded so easily where I had failed. So the truth is that at our first meeting I was not at all disposed to like Miss Elizabeth Stanton. She seemed far too full of herself for my liking.

"You just wait till I tell Mama and Papa about Kaspar," she went on. "Can I take him downstairs to show them?"

It hadn't even occurred to me until that moment that this little girl could blow the whole secret. I crouched down so that we were face to face and put my hands on her shoulders. She had to know just how serious I was about this. "You can't. You can't say a word," I told her. "The thing is, you see, I'm not allowed to keep pets up here. Against the rules, see? No pets in the servants' quarters. If anyone finds out, I'll get the sack, lose my position. I'll have nowhere to live, and neither will Kaspar. No one else knows he lives up here. So you won't tell anyone, will you? It'll be our little secret, right?"

She was looking at me very intently all the while. She thought for a moment or two. Then she said: "I don't like rules, especially unfair rules like not being allowed to keep a cat. So I won't tell anyone, cross my heart and hope to die." Then she added, "But you will let me come up and feed Kaspar again sometime, won't you?"

I hadn't any choice.

"I suppose so," I said. "If you want to."

"I do, I do," she cried. "I like him so much, and he likes me, I know he does."

It was true. Kaspar was looking up at her adoringly. He could hardly take his eyes off her. She grabbed my hand and shook it. "Oh thank you, thank you. But I don't know your name, do I?"

"Johnny Trott," I told her. She let out a peal of laughter. "Johnny Rot. Johnny Rot. That's such a funny name. Bye Kaspar, bye Johnny Rot." And still giggling she skipped off down the corridor and was gone. As I watched her go I remembered the last person who had found my name so funny. I was already disliking Elizabeth a little less.

I had no idea then and I still have no idea now how she managed to get Kaspar to eat his liver that morning. I asked her later on, once I'd got to know her better, and she gave me one of her infuriating shrugs. "S'easy when you know how," she told me. "Animals always do whatever I want, because they know I'd do anything for them, and that's because they know I love them, and that's why they love me." She had this way, as some children do, of making everything sound so simple and straightforward.

After that first surprise visit, Miss Elizabeth Stanton, or Lizziebeth as I discovered she liked to be called, came up to my room to feed Kaspar at least twice a day without fail. Sometimes I was there, sometimes I wasn't. Whenever she'd been I'd find a little scribbled note on my pillow. It would say something like this:

"Dear Jonny Rot, I came to feed Caspa again. I stoll some smoked samon from my breakfast. He likes it a lot which I don't because it smells of fish wich is horrible. I made your bed too which you didn't. And you should too. Don worry your secrets safe. Promise. I like secrits because its like hidding and I like hidding. from your friend Lizziebeth."

There's no doubt at all in my mind that it was the arrival of Lizziebeth that saved Kaspar's life. Somehow she brought joy into his life where there had only been sorrow. With her there beside him he was eating and drinking everything that was put in front of him. Within a week he was beginning to sharpen his claws, mostly on the curtains, but sometimes on my trousers, and when I was wearing them too. That hurt a lot. I didn't mind much, though, because I was just so happy to see him getting better. His coat shone, his tail swished, and when one day he smiled up at me I knew for sure that Prince Kaspar Kandinsky was himself again. Lizziebeth had lifted his spirits, and she'd lifted mine too. But I was worried that one day she might "let the cat out of the bag", so to speak. I kept reminding her that secrecy was everything.

"Remember, Lizziebeth, you've got to keep schtum," I told her one evening, tapping my nose conspiratorially. She liked that. So whenever she left my room after that, she'd tap her nose. "Schtum," she'd whisper. "I've got to keep schtum."

Lizziebeth became quite a little mascot on our corridor, and quite a hero too on account of everything she'd done for Kaspar. She may have been a little bit on the talkative side, and could be quite mischievous too – she was a bundle of fun and she made us all laugh. But I couldn't help wondering whether she might one day become too overexcited and blurt out our secret by mistake.

I took all the precautions I could, asking her to always check behind her before she climbed the stairs to our corridor, and I made it an absolute rule that she spoke in whispers whenever she came to see us. Those, it seemed, were the kind of rules she was quite happy with. Lizziebeth liked anything, I discovered, that involved some kind of conspiracy. It was during these long whispered conversations in my room that I got to know so much more about her. Actually, to begin with they weren't conversations at all, not as such. They were more like monologues. Once Lizziebeth started one of her stories, there was no stopping her. "Do you know…" she'd begin, and on she'd go, on and on. She'd sit there cross-legged on the floor of my room with Kaspar on her lap and just talk and talk. And I'd be happy to listen, because she told me of a world I'd never seen inside before. For over a year now, ever since I'd left the orphanage, I'd served people like her at the Savoy; fetched and carried for them, polished their boots, brushed their coats,

opened doors for them, bowed and scraped, as bell-boys have to do. But until now not one of them had ever really talked to me, unless they were snapping their fingers at me, or ordering me to do something.

It's true that I wasn't sure sometimes whether Lizziebeth was talking to me or to Kaspar. It didn't much matter either way. Both of us would listen as entranced as the other, Kaspar gazing up into her eyes all the while, purring with pleasure, and me hanging on her every word.

Once she told us about the great ship she'd come over on from America, about the icebergs she'd seen, as tall as the skyscrapers in New York, which was where she lived, how one day when they were at sea she'd wandered off on her own to find somewhere to hide, and found herself right down below in the engine room. There was quite a kerfuffle, she said, because everyone thought she'd fallen overboard. When at last she was found and brought back to their cabin her mother had cried and cried, and called her "my little angel", but her father had told her she was "the naughtiest girl in the whole world". So she wasn't sure *what* she was.

Afterwards they had taken her to the Captain of the ship who had a great, fat face and sad eyes, like a walrus she said, and they'd made her apologise for causing so much trouble to the crew who had been searching for her all over the ship for two hours before she was found, and to the Captain who'd had to stop the ship in mid-ocean, and had lookouts scanning the ocean with binoculars looking for her. She had to promise faithfully in front of the Captain never to go off on her own while they were on the ship. She promised with her fingers crossed behind her, she said, so it didn't count. So when it got rough a day

or two later and they were being tossed about in
the biggest, greenest waves she'd ever seen, and
everyone was as sick as dogs, she decided she'd
do what one of the sailors had told her to do if it

ever got rough, to go down to the very bottom of the ship where the boat doesn't roll so much, and just lie down. The very bottom of the ship, she discovered, was full of cows and calves. So she lay down beside them in the straw, and that was where they found her, fast asleep, when the storm was over. This time they were *both* "mad" with her. So she was locked in the cabin as a punishment. She shrugged. "I didn't care," she told me. "Who gives a fig, anyway?"

Back at home in New York her governess was always sending her up to her room to make her do her writing all over again, or because her spelling wasn't good enough. She was always being sent to her room by her mother too, for running around the house when she should walk, or making a noise when her father was working in his study. "I didn't mind," she said, with a shrug and a little laugh. "I didn't give a fig, anyway." In the holidays the family

would sail up the coast to Maine in their three-masted yacht, which was called the *Abe Lincoln*, and they'd live in this big house on an island where there was no other house but theirs, and no one there except them, their guests and the servants. One day she decided to be a pirate, so she tied a spotted pirate's scarf around her head and went off with a spade to look for buried treasure. And when they came calling for her she hid away in a cave, and she only came out when she was good and ready. She knew they'd be mad at her, but she really didn't like anyone calling for her "like I was some kind of a dog". So when she strolled back into the house that evening, she was sent straight up to bed without any dinner. "I didn't want any dinner anyway," she said, "so I didn't give a fig, anyway, did I?"

Bit by bit, through these stories and dozens of others, I pieced together something of the lives of

Lizziebeth and her family. I looked at them now with very different eyes whenever they walked by me on their way into breakfast, whenever I opened the door for them or wished them good morning. Lizziebeth would give me a great beaming smile whenever she saw me in the lobby, and Mr Freddie would wink at me from the front door, and sometimes he'd *miaow* softly as he passed me by. Such moments were enough to lift my spirits all day long. Life was suddenly good, and fun too. Kaspar was well again, we had both found a new friend, and our secret was safe. Everything was fine, or so I thought.

Running Wild

Everything after that seemed to happen suddenly, and in very quick succession. It was a quiet weekend at the hotel, with fewer guests around. There were no big dressy dinners, no grand balls, no smart parties. All of us who worked there preferred it like this, even if the days could drag a bit. Everyone was more relaxed. I liked the weekends anyway, because Kaspar and I usually saw more of Lizziebeth then. She'd be bored out of her mind downstairs, and would often sneak up to see Kaspar, sometimes three or four times a day, leaving me a note each time. I finished work earlier on a Sunday, so usually she'd be up there in my room with Kaspar, waiting for me when I got back. Sometimes she'd steal away some scones and cake, hiding them away in a napkin – she was always saying I was too thin and needed feeding up – and since I was always more than a little hungry after work, I didn't argue with her.

We were sitting there one Sunday evening tucking into some delicious fruit cake, when I heard a voice in the corridor outside. Skullface! It was Skullface! She was talking to Mary O'Connell, and she was not in a good mood.

"That idiot boy, Johnny Trott, is he in?"

"I haven't seen him, Mrs Blaise," Mary told her. "Honest."

The footsteps came closer and closer, the bunch of keys rattling louder with every step.

Skullface was ranting now. "Do you know what that he's gone and done? Well, I'll tell you, shall I? He's only used a black brush on Lord Macauley's best brown boots. There's black all over them. And who gets the blame? Me. Well. I'll have his guts for garters, I will. Where is he?"

"I don't know, Mrs Blaise, honest to God I don't." Mary was doing her best for me.

The footsteps were right outside my door now, and there I was with Lizziebeth in my room, and Kaspar cleaning himself on her lap. All she had to do was to open the door and I'd get the sack for sure. I could hear my heart pounding in my ears. I was praying that somehow, anyhow, Mary would prevent her from opening that door. It was this very moment that Kaspar chose to stop washing his paws and spring out of Lizziebeth's lap, yowling in his fury. It wasn't his gentle *miaow*, this was his wailing war cry, and it was shrill and loud, horribly loud. For a moment or two there was silence outside the door. Then, "A cat! As I live and breathe, a cat!" cried Skullface. "Johnny Trott's got a cat in his room! How dare he? How dare he? It's against the rules, my rules!"

I looked aghast at Lizziebeth. Without a moment's hesitation she picked up Kaspar, and dumped him unceremoniously in my arms. "In the wardrobe," she whispered. "Get in the wardrobe. Quick!"

Once in there I crouched down, stroking Kaspar frantically to calm him down, to stop him from yowling again. Then I heard something I simply couldn't believe. Kaspar was yowling again, from outside the wardrobe, from my room. Yet he couldn't be, because he was with me, inside the wardrobe, in my arms and he definitely wasn't yowling. Yet he *was* yowling – I could hear him! In my panic and confusion it took several moments before I realised what was going on: Lizziebeth was out there in my room and mimicking Kaspar pitch perfectly.

Mary told me afterwards – she told everyone afterwards – exactly what had happened. Apparently Lizziebeth opened the door to Skullface yowling and wailing at her just like Kaspar. Skullface just stood there, gaping at Lizziebeth. She could not believe her eyes. It was a while before she could speak at all. Her mouth opened and shut like a goldfish, Mary said. Then Skullface gathered herself a little. "What on earth, young lady…" she said at last. "What on earth do you think you are doing up here in the servants' quarters, young lady? It's strictly out of bounds."

Lizziebeth yowled back at her. "I'm a cat," she said quite calmly, in between yowls. "I was chasing a mouse, and he ran in here. So I ran in after him and I caught him. I'm very good at catching mice, you know. I gobbled him up, just like that. One gulp. I've got to tell you, he tasted just wonderful. Best mouse I ever ate. Byeee!" With that, she yowled at the astonished Skullface, and skipped off down the corridor, still yowling as she went, past Skullface, past Mary and the others, all of whom by now had come out into the corridor to see what all the fuss was about.

Skullface, it seems, then stuck her head round my door, took one quick look into the room, slammed the door furiously behind her, and stormed off down the corridor, fulminating as she went.

"Children, wretched children!" she fumed. "If I had my way they wouldn't be allowed in the Savoy at all. Nothing but a nuisance, a perfect nuisance. If there's one thing I can't stand it's a spoilt child. And an American spoilt child is the worst of all, the work of the devil himself! Running wild like that all over my hotel. How dare she?" She stopped and turned round, wagging her finger at everyone. "And you tell that Johnny Trott when you see him that he will apologise to Lord Macauley, and polish his boots again. This time I want them nutty brown and shining, not a trace of black, and he's to come and show them to me before he returns them to his lordship. At once, at once. You tell him."

How we laughed in the corridor when she'd gone. We were doubled up and aching with it. Lizziebeth, who was already a great favourite with everyone up there, had now become a matchless heroine to us all. Her quick thinking, her brazenness and her fearlessness had saved the day, probably saved my job too, and most certainly saved Kaspar from being taken away.

But it was only the next day that this same fearlessness very nearly cost her her life, and mine too, come to that. It was from Kaspar that I first learned something was wrong. He was always happy to see me when I came upstairs after work. He'd be lying there on the bed, his legs in the air, his tail swishing, willing me to tickle his tummy. I came back to my room to see him at about eleven o'clock, my usual time, my first work-break of the morning. I was hoping Lizziebeth might be there with him. But this morning she wasn't. And neither was Kaspar lying on my bed. Instead he was pacing the room and yowling. He was in a very agitated state, leaping up and down and off the windowsill. I'd seen him do this before if there was a pigeon strutting up and cooing at him from the parapet outside the window. But there was no pigeon. I tried feeding Kaspar – I thought it might calm him down – but he wasn't interested. Clearly nothing mattered to him except whatever was going on outside that window. So I climbed up, and opened the window wide enough for me to crane my neck, so I could see all the way along the narrow gully in both directions. No pigeons there either.

That was when I spotted Lizziebeth. I could see at once what she was trying to do. She was on her hands and knees and climbing out of the gully up on to the roof tiles. Ahead of her was a pigeon, hopping ever upwards on one leg towards the ridge of the roof. Its other leg hung useless. Lizziebeth was following it, cooing as she climbed, stopping from time to time to throw it some crumbs, trying all she could to entice it down. She seemed quite unaware of the danger she was in.

My first instinct was to shout to her, to warn her, but something told me that to alarm her at that moment was the worst thing I could do. Instead, I climbed out of the window, closing it behind me so that Kaspar couldn't follow me, and crept along the gully trying not to look down over the parapet and down into the street, eight storeys below. Lizziebeth had almost reached the ridge above me, but by now the pigeon was hopping away from her along the ridge towards the chimney stack. I climbed up after her. Only when I was right below her did I venture to call out to her, and then only as softly as I could.

"Lizziebeth," I said. "It's me. It's Johnny. I'm right below you. You mustn't go any higher. You mustn't."

She didn't look down at first. She just kept climbing.

"It's the pigeon," she told me. "He's awful hurt. Looks like he's broke his leg or something."

That was the moment she looked down. Only then did she realise just how high she was. All her fearlessness left her in an instant. She slipped at once and clung there, frozen with terror. The ridge was only a short distance above her, but I could see that she wasn't going to be able to get up there on her own, not now, and that there was no possible way she could come down either.

"Stay right where you are, Lizziebeth," I told her, "Don't move, I'm coming up."

All I could think of was that somehow I had to get her up on to that ridge. We'd just sit there until we were seen and rescue came. But between me and her was a steep, tiled roof, acres of tiles, it seemed, and with no foothold, nothing to hold on to.

One slip, one loose tile, and I'd be slipping and sliding back down the roof and probably over the parapet. It didn't bear thinking about. So I tried not to. That was why I talked to her all the way up as I climbed. I wasn't only trying to calm her fears, I was desperately trying to calm my own.

"Just hang on, Lizziebeth. Look up at the pigeon.
Whatever you do, don't look down. I'm coming.
I'll be right there. Promise."

I climbed as fast as my shaking legs would allow.
I went sideways across the tiles like a crab,
zigzagging up the roof. It was longer, but it made it

easier, safer, less steep. I just fixed my mind on reaching that ridge, and climbed. More than once I dislodged a tile and sent it crashing down into the gulley below. Then at last I was up there and sitting astride the ridge. Now I was able to reach down, grasp Lizziebeth by the wrist and haul her up. We sat there facing one another, safe for the moment, but both of us breathless with fear. The pigeon was quite oblivious to all that had been done to help him. He hopped one-legged back down the roof, along the gully, and then up on to the parapet, pecking away at the crumbs as he went. He flew off quite happily.

Someone must have been watching all this drama unfold, because the Fire Brigade came soon enough. There were bells clanging in the street below, and firemen in shiny helmets began to appear all along the gully below, one of them talking to us all the while, telling us again and again not to move. The truth is that neither of us could have moved even if we'd wanted to. They ran ladders up to us and lifted us down, Lizziebeth first. When at last I was carried in through the big window at the end of our corridor, I saw it was crowded with people. The hotel manager was there, Skullface, Mary, Luke, Mr Freddie, everyone. As I walked by they all began to clap me on the back. It was only then that I really understood what I'd done. The manager pumped my hand, and told me I was a proper little hero. But Skullface wasn't clapping. She wasn't smiling either. She knew something wasn't quite as it should be, but I could tell she didn't know what it was. I smiled at her though, defiantly, triumphantly. I think I enjoyed that moment more than all the backslapping and handshaking. Although that was fun too.

They laid on a celebratory supper for me down in the kitchens that night, and sat me at the head of the table. They sang *For He's a Jolly Good Fellow* over and over again. We had quite a night of it. After a while the manager came to fetch me away. He was taking me up to the Stantons' rooms, he told me, because the family wanted to thank me personally. When I was ushered in, I found the three of them lined up in the sitting room to greet me, Lizziebeth in her dressing gown. It was all very formal and proper. I stood before them, trying all I could not to catch Lizziebeth's eye. I knew that just one look between us could give everything away.

"Young man," Mr Stanton began. "Mrs Stanton and I, but most of all Elizabeth of course, owe you a very great debt of gratitude."

Suddenly I saw, and I could not have been more surprised, that there were tears in his eyes, and his voice broke. I had never imagined that men such as this could ever cry.

"Elizabeth is our only child," he went on, his

voice charged with emotion. "She is very precious to us, and today you saved her life. We shall not forget this."

He stepped forward, shook my hand, and presented me with a large white envelope.

"No money could ever be enough of course, young man, but this is just a token of our deep appreciation for what you did, for your extraordinary courage."

I took the envelope from him, and opened it. In it were five ten pound notes. I had never in my life seen so much money. Before I could say thank you, or indeed say anything at all, Lizziebeth was standing there in front of me, holding out a large piece of paper. I was looking down at a picture of Kaspar.

"I drew it for you," she said. She was speaking to me as if we hardly knew one another. She was an amazing actress. "I like drawing pictures. It's a cat. I hope you like it. I did it for you because I especially like black cats. And on the other side, you can see…" She turned the paper over for me. "On the other side I've done a picture of the ship we're sailing home on next week. It's got four big funnels, and Papa says it's the biggest, fastest ship in the whole wide world. It's true, isn't it, Papa?"

"She's called the *Titanic*," Mrs Stanton added. "It'll be her maiden voyage, you know. Isn't she the most magnificent ship you ever saw?"

Stowaway

$\mathcal{I}$ should have taken more notice of Lizziebeth's drawings, appreciated them more when she gave them to me, and afterwards, but the truth was I'd never in my life seen so much money. Sitting on my bed late that night, I kept counting it to make sure I wasn't dreaming it. Everyone on the corridor came in. They had to see it with their own eyes.

Mary O'Connell held each note up to the light, I remember, to check it wasn't a forgery. "Well, you never know, do you? Not with these rich folk," she said. I told Mary something I hadn't spoken about with the others, how I'd been thinking about it and was beginning to feel very uncomfortable about taking the money. Mary was always good about right and wrong, she understood these things.

"I didn't do it for the money, Mary." I told her, "I did it because it was Lizziebeth up there."

"I know that, Johnny," she said. "But that doesn't mean you don't deserve it, does it? This money is your ticket out of here. It's a God-given fortune, so it is. There's two years wages here. For God's sakes, you could go anywhere, do anything. Wouldn't any one of us like to do that! You don't want to be having to shine shoes for the rest of your life, do you?"

I lay awake most of that night talking it all

through with Kaspar – he was a good listener. By morning I felt that despite everything Mary had said, I might have to give the money back. Lizziebeth's drawings were a thank you, and that was fine; but I couldn't help thinking that the money was in some way a kind of pay-off; reward money for a bell-boy. No, I didn't like being treated like a bell-boy, and I didn't want a reward. I'd give the money back. But then by morning I'd almost changed my mind again. Maybe Mary had been right after all. I'd keep the money. Why shouldn't I?

I was still lying there propped up on my pillows, with Kaspar curled up at the end of the bed, looking at Lizziebeth's picture of the great ship with the four funnels steaming through the ocean, gulls flying overhead, when the door suddenly flew open. Skullface stood there. "I thought so. I thought as much!" she said. "First that girl was in here *miaow*ing like a cat, and that was odd enough. Then

a day later she was up here again, wasn't she? But this time up on the roof, just outside your window. Strange that. Strange sort of coincidence, I thought. D'you know something, Johnny Trott, I don't believe in coincidences. And now you're quite the little hero, aren't you? Well, I weren't born yesterday. I'm no one's fool, Johnny Trott. I knew something fishy was going on. But now I can see, it weren't fishy at all, it were catty, more like."

She came into the room, shutting the door behind her, and stood over me, a nasty vindictive grin on her face. Kaspar had leaped on to the window-sill, and was hissing and wailing at her furiously "Well now," she went on. "I hear you've come into the money, Johnny Trott, is that right?" I nodded.

"Here's the deal then," she went on. "Either you pack your bags, hand in your uniform and you're out in the streets within the hour, or you hand over the money. It's that simple. Hand over the money and you can stay. I'll even let you keep your horrible cat up here, for a while anyway. There, I can't be more generous than that, can I now?"

A few moments later as she walked out of my room, tucking the envelope into her pocket, I was almost grateful to her. After all she'd made my decision for me. I sat down on my bed where Kaspar soon joined me for some petting and reassurance. I was thinking things through. I was no

poorer than I had been before it all happened. And now at least I had her word, for what it was worth, that Kaspar would be safe, for a while anyway. I still had my job. I felt a great sense of relief, but that was very soon overwhelmed by a wave of sadness. All too soon now Lizziebeth would be leaving and sailing back to America. "I'm going to miss her. We're both going to miss her, Kaspar," I said aloud. "We won't miss the money – we never really had it, did we – but we will miss Lizziebeth. What are we going to do without her?"

I shouldn't have said anything. Kaspar must have understood enough of it or maybe he just picked up on my sadness, I don't know. But either way, it became clear to me as the days passed that he understood all too well that Lizziebeth would soon be going. After the very public rooftop rescue – it had been in all the papers too – Lizziebeth had the perfect excuse now to come up and see me often, even for us to be seen talking down in the lobby. So at least we were able to spend more and more time together during those final days.

Time and again I was tempted to tell her about

how Skullface had blackmailed me and taken her father's money, but I thought how angry it would make her, that it was too much to expect a young girl of that age to keep quiet about such a thing. So I didn't tell her anything about that, but I did tell her things I'd never told anyone else: about my life in the orphanage in Islington, about Harry, the cockroach that I'd kept as a pet in a matchbox, about Mr Wellington, who was supposed to look after us, but who must have hated children so much because he'd cane us so often for the slightest thing. He caned me for keeping Harry, then took him away and stamped on him right in front of my eyes, in front of all of us. That was what made me run away in the end – I'd often thought of it before, but never dared. I told her how

I'd wandered the streets of London for weeks, living rough, before finding work as a bell-boy at the Savoy. And of course she wanted to know all about Countess Kandinsky. I told her my dream of finding my mother one day. I told her so many of my hopes and dreams. And all the while, she listened wide-eyed.

That last week together, things changed between Lizziebeth and me. From the moment we were sitting up on that roof holding hands, and sharing our fear, she was no longer a little rich girl from America, and I wasn't a fourteen-year-old orphan from London. We had become proper friends, the best of friends. She no longer gabbled on all the time about herself, or about Kaspar, as she had when I'd first known her. She asked questions, and she wanted answers. "We haven't got much more time together," she said one morning, "so you have to tell me everything, because I want to remember everything about you and about Kaspar for ever and ever."

She'd bring me new drawings every day, of her house in New York, of the Statue of Liberty, of her island home in Maine, of her dressed as a pirate, of her with Kaspar, of me in my uniform, but mostly of Kaspar: Kaspar sleeping, Kaspar sitting, Kaspar hunting. But as the day for her to leave came ever closer, we became more silent together, more sad together. She would hug Kaspar close all the time she was with us in my room, and I could feel her wanting to stretch every minute into an hour, into a week, into a month. I wanted the same.

It was on the last evening that she first suggested the idea. She was cradling Kaspar, rocking him gently, her head buried in his neck, when suddenly she looked up at me, her eyes filled with tears.

"You could come, Johnny. You and Kaspar, you could come with us. We could go on the ship together. You could come and live in New York. You'd love it. I know you would. And in America you wouldn't have to be a bell-boy. In America you can be whatever you want to be, that's what Papa says. It's the land of the free. You could be President of the United States. Anyone could be. Please come, Johnny, please come." As she was talking I felt a sudden hope surging

inside me at the prospect of a new and exciting life across the ocean, in America, but immediately I could see how impossible it was.

"I can't, Lizziebeth," I said. "I mean I couldn't even pay for my passage..."

"What about the money?" she replied. "What about the money my father gave you?"

I told her everything, all about how Skullface had blackmailed me. I hadn't intended to. It just came pouring out.

Lizziebeth was silent for a while.

"She's a witch," she said finally, "and I hate her." Then she brightened suddenly. "I could ask Papa," she went on. "He's got a lot of money. He could pay for your passage."

"No," I told her firmly. "I don't want money from him."

She looked hurt and crestfallen at this, and I wished at once I hadn't spoken so directly.

"You don't want to come, do you?" She said.

"I do," I told her. "I really do. I don't want to be carrying luggage and polishing shoes all my life, do I? And I'd love to go across to America in that big ship you drew for me – what was it called again?"

"*Titanic,*" Lizziebeth said, in tears now. "We're going early in the morning. We've got to go by train first, Ma says, before we can get to the ship. You could come with us. You could come and see us off. And you could bring Kaspar."

"I suppose I could see the ship then, couldn't I?" I said, but I knew even as I spoke that I was grasping at straws. "It's no good, Lizziebeth. Skullface wouldn't let me have a day off work. I know she wouldn't. I'd really like to see the *Titanic* too. Is it really the biggest ship in the world?"

"And the fastest," she said, getting up suddenly and handing me Kaspar. "I'm going to speak to Papa. You saved my life didn't you? I'm going to ask him, and I'm going to tell him about Skullface too."

She was out of my room and gone before I could stop her.

The very same day, only a few hours later, Skullface was seen walking grimfaced out of the tradesmen's entrance with her suitcase, "never to return", as Mr Freddie told me with a smile all over his face. But I never saw my money again.

The next morning I found myself sitting in a first class train carriage with the Stanton family on the way to Southampton. The manager had told me that he'd had a special request from Mr Stanton that Kaspar and I be allowed to accompany the family to Southampton, and help them with their luggage on board ship. He said that considering recent events, and how I had enhanced the good name of the hotel, he was happy this one time to let me go. But I would be on duty, he reminded me. I had to wear my Savoy uniform, carry all their trunks and bags on board, and see to their every need until the ship sailed.

In among the luggage I carried out of the hotel that day was a picnic basket Mary O'Connell had "borrowed" from the stores. Inside the basket was Kaspar. He yowled all the way down in the lift, wailed all the way across the lobby, past Mr Freddie, who lifted his hat to him in farewell. He only stopped his complaining once we were in the cab, when Lizziebeth took him out and cradled him in her arms. That was when she began telling her mother and father the whole story of our secret, of how we'd met, all about Kaspar and me, and the Countess Kandinsky, and my orphanage, and Harry the cockroach and Mr Wellington, and how I'd run away. One story flowed into the next, my whole life story and Kaspar's in a torrent of words that tumbled over one another in her excitement to tell the whole thing. She hardly paused for breath until we got to the station.

Kaspar sat on Lizziebeth's lap all the way down on the train to Southampton. It was for the most part a silent journey, because Lizziebeth slept and so did Kasper.

I shall never forget my first sighting of the *Titanic*. She seemed to dwarf the entire dockside. As I went up the gangplank carrying the Stantons' trunks, Lizziebeth in front of me carrying Kaspar in the picnic basket, the band was playing on the quayside, and there were crowds of people everywhere, spectators on shore and passengers all along the railings, high excitement and anticipation on every face. I was agog with it all. Twice or three times I went back and forth to their cabin – deck C, number 52. I've never forgotten the number. Their cabin was at least as spacious as their rooms at the Savoy, and just as luxurious. I was bowled over by the palatial splendour of everything I saw, by the sheer enormity of the ship, both inside and out. It was grander and more magnificent than I could ever have imagined.

The time came when I'd carried all their trunks up to their cabin, and I knew the moment for parting had come. Lizziebeth knew it too. Sitting on the sofa, she said her last goodbye to Kaspar, burying her face in his neck and sobbing her heart out. Her father took the cat from her as gently as he could and put him back in the picnic basket. It was as he was doing this that I decided. It had never even occurred to me until that moment.

"Lizziebeth," I said, "I want you to take him with you to America."

"You mean it?" she cried. "You really mean it?"

"I mean it," I told her.

Lizziebeth turned to her mother and father. "I can, can't I, Ma? Please Papa. Say yes, please."

Neither objected. On the contrary, they looked delighted.

Each of them shook me by the hand. They were still reserved, but I saw a genuine kindness there, and a warmth in their eyes that I had not seen before. I crouched down and stroked Kaspar in his picnic basket. He looked up at me very intently. He knew what was happening, that we were saying goodbye. Lizziebeth led me to the door of the cabin. She clung to me for so long that I thought she'd never let go. The ship's siren was sounding. I broke away from her and ran up on to the deck, brushing away my tears.

I've thought a lot about this since, about why I gave Kaspar away like that, on the spur of the moment, and about what I did next too. I remember standing there on deck with everyone waving, with the siren blasting and the band playing, and I knew then I couldn't go back to my old life, to my little attic room at the Savoy, that I should stay with Kaspar and Lizziebeth, and that I just didn't want to leave the ship, this wonderful ship, this magical floating palace. When the final call went out for any last visitors and porters to leave the ship, I stayed on board. It was that simple. I ran to the rail and began waving with all the other passengers. I was one of them. I was going. I was going to America, to Lizziebeth's land of the free, where I could be anything I wanted to be. It really wasn't until I saw the *Titanic* moving away from the dockside and saw the widening gap of sea in between, that I realised quite what I had done, what a momentous decision I had made, that there was no going back. I was a stowaway on the *Titanic*.

"We've Only Gone and Hit A Flaming Iceberg"

My life as a stowaway didn't last long. It took me a while to understand that I was in the First Class part of the ship; and when I did, I discovered it wasn't at all easy to blend in with the First Class passengers all around me. Everyone was in their travelling finery, and dressed as I was in my uniform of a Savoy bell-boy, I stuck out like a sore thumb. They even moved differently, as if they belonged there, as if they had all the time in the world. Maybe you need a lifetime to learn how to look nonchalantly wealthy.

For a while the uniform actually helped. I could pass myself off as a steward, and of course that was easy enough for me. I knew well enough how to touch my forelock, how to help old ladies down the stairs, how to point out to people where to go – even if I hadn't a clue where anything was. For the first hour or so, as the other passengers promenaded the deck, exploring the ship, that was what I did too, until I began getting some strange looks from some of the crew and the other stewards who clearly thought my uniform a bit strange. I knew that sooner or later

I'd be rumbled, that my luck couldn't hold out for long if I went on pretending to be one of them. I also realised that if I stayed in First Class I was bound to bump into one of the Stanton family, and I wasn't at all sure how they would respond if they discovered that I had stowed away. I could see the steerage passengers all crowded on the lower deck at the stern end of the ship. They were more my own kind I thought, I'd be safer there. So that's where I headed. I took off my tunic and cap, and when no one was looking dropped them over the side.

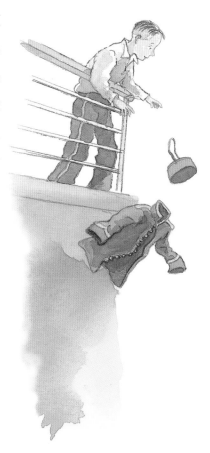

Then I vaulted over the rail, and tried to mingle in
among the steerage passengers as best I could.

We were well out to sea by now, the last of England
fast disappearing over the horizon. The sea was flat
calm, like a silver blue lake. No one was paying me
any attention. They were all enjoying themselves far
too much to know I was even there. You only had to
use your eyes and ears to know that these steerage
passengers came from all over the world. There were
Irish, Chinese, French, Germans, Americans and quite
a few London cockneys too. I was feeling much more
at home already. I went below deck, and after a long
search, at last, found myself an empty berth in a
dormitory at the bottom of the ship. There were a few
men in there, but they paid me little attention.

I was lying down, my hands behind my head, my
eyes closed, the ship's engines throbbing through
me, believing absolutely I had got away with it,
when everything went badly wrong.

I heard voices, loud voices, voices of authority. I opened my eyes and saw two sailors coming through the dormitory. "We're looking for a stowaway. Have you seen him? He's kind of a Japanese-looking fellow." One of them stopped by a table where some men were sat about playing cards. "Has he come through here? Little fellow he is. We know he's down here somewhere."

I think I would have been fine if I hadn't panicked. I could have just pretended to be asleep. I didn't look Japanese. They wouldn't have bothered me. But I didn't think. I got up and ran, and they came after me hollering at me to stop. I took the stairs to the deck three at a time. Once up there I hid in the first place I found – of course it was the most obvious, and therefore the most stupid place I could ever have chosen – a lifeboat. Inside I saw the Japanese man sitting at the far end, knees drawn up under his chin, rocking back and forth and gnawing at his knuckles. And that was where, only minutes later the two of us were discovered, caught like rats in a trap. We were not treated at all kindly as we were hustled along the decks, but at least I felt we had the sympathy of the steerage passengers. All the booing and jeering seemed directed more at our sailor escorts than at us. Both of us were taken before the Captain – Captain Smith he was called – and there were three other men there already. So there were five of us in all, all stowaways, an Italian I remember who spoke very little English, the Japanese man and three Englishmen, myself among them. From behind his desk the Captain looked at us wearily out of deep-set, sad eyes. With his great beard and calm bearing, he looked every inch a sea captain. He didn't curse us or berate us as the sailors had.

"Well Mr Lightoller," he said, to the officer standing beside him. "So, we've got five of them, have we? Not as many as I'd feared. What shall we do with them then? Where do we need them most, would you say?"

"Down below in the engine room, Captain," the officer replied. "Stokers. We're short of a dozen stokers at least. And if you want to make full speed as you say, if you want to make the crossing in record time, as you say, then we could do with them down below. Looking at them, I'd say they were a bit on the thin and spindly side, but there's nothing we can do about that."

The Captain looked right at me. "Why did you do it?" he asked me.

I told him the truth, part of it anyway. I had nothing to lose. "Because I didn't want to leave the ship, sir. She's so beautiful, and everyone says she's very fast too. And I've never been on a ship before."

"Well, I have, son," laughed the Captain. "Dozens of them. And you're right, this one is fast, the fastest ship that ever sailed, and what's more she's unsinkable too. Very well, Mr Lightoller, you will set these men to work their passage to New York as stokers. It will be hot work and hard, gentlemen, and for this you will be fed and looked after well enough. Take them away."

So began the hardest three days I have ever worked in all my life. My body never ached so much, every bone, every muscle, every joint. My hands never bled so much either, open blisters on every finger. I was never so hot and dirty, never so completely and utterly exhausted. The stokers about me were strong men, big men, muscle-bound and sinewy. Stripped to the waist as we were I felt like a sparrow among eagles. The pounding thunder of the engines in my ears was deafening, the blast of the furnaces scorched my skin. But for all this discomfort I somehow found it the most exciting and invigorating place I had ever been. Every time I looked up and saw those great boilers, those great pistons driving, I marvelled at them, at the power and the beauty of it all. And believe it or not, as I shovelled coal for hour after hour in that stifling heat, there was only one thought that kept me shovelling: it was *me* driving these mighty engines, Johnny Trott. I wasn't just a bell-boy anymore. I was a man among men, and our muscles were firing the boilers that were powering the engines that were turning the screws that were driving the fastest ship the world had ever seen across the Atlantic. I felt proud of the work I was doing.

My fellow stokers ribbed me mercilessly from time to time, for I was the baby among them. I didn't mind. They ribbed the little Japanese man too till they discovered that, small though he was, he could shovel more coal than any of us. He was called Michiya, but we all called him Little Mitch – and he was little, littler even than me. Maybe because we had been fellow stowaways, or maybe because we were both about the same size, he became quite a friend.

He spoke no English at all, so we conversed in gestures and smiles. We managed to make ourselves well enough understood. Like the rest of them I was black from head to toe after every shift. But Captain Smith was true to his word, we were all well enough looked after. We had plenty of hot water to wash ourselves clean, we had all the food we could eat and a warm bunk to sleep in. I didn't go up on deck that much. It was a long way up, and when I did have an hour or two off I found I was just too tired to do anything much except sleep. Down there in the bowels of the ship I didn't know if it was night or day – and I didn't much care either. It was just work, sleep, eat, work, sleep, eat. I was too tired even to dream.

When I did go up on deck I looked out on a moonlit sea, or a sunlit sea, that was always as flat as a pond and shining. I never saw another ship, just the wide horizons. Occasionally there were birds soaring over the decks, and once to everyone's great excitement we spotted dozens of leaping dolphins. I had never known such beauty. Every time I went up on deck though, I was drawn towards the First Class part of the ship. I'd stay there by the rail for a while, hoping against hope I might see Lizziebeth come walking by with Kaspar on his lead.

But I never saw them. I thought of them though as I shovelled and sweated, as I lay in my bunk in between shifts, as I looked over that glassy sea. I kept trying to summon up the courage to climb over the railings and find my way again back to their cabin. I longed to see the look of surprise on Lizziebeth's face when she saw I was on board. I knew how pleased she'd be to see me, that Kaspar would swish his tail and smile up at me. But about Lizziebeth's mother and father I couldn't be at all sure. The truth is that I still believed they would think badly of me for stowing away as I had.

I decided that it would be better to wait until we got to New York, and then I'd just walk up to them all and surprise them on the quayside. I'd tell them then and there that I'd taken Lizziebeth's advice and come to live in America, in the land of the free. They'd never need to know I'd stowed away.

I was half sleeping, half dreaming in my bunk, dreaming that Kaspar was yowling at me, trying to wake me. We were in some kind of danger and he was trying to warn me. Then it happened. The ship suddenly shuddered and shook. I sat up. Right away it felt to me like some kind of a collision, and I could tell it had happened on the starboard side. A long silence followed. Then I heard a great rushing and roaring of escaping steam, like a death rattle. I knew that something had gone terribly wrong, that the ship had been wounded. The engines had stopped.

Half a dozen of us got dressed at once and rushed up to the third deck, the boat deck. We all expected to see the ship we had collided with, because that was what we thought had happened. But we could see nothing, no ship, nothing but the stars and an empty sea all around. There was no one else on deck except us. It was as if no one else had felt it, as if it had all been a bad dream. No one else had woken, so it followed that nothing had happened. I was almost beginning to believe I had imagined the whole thing, when I saw Little Mitch come rushing along the deck towards us carrying something in both hands. It was a huge piece of ice shaped like a giant tooth, jagged and sharp. He was shouting the same thing over and over again, but I couldn't understand him, none of us could. Then one of the other stokers said it. "Iceberg! It's off an iceberg! We've only gone and hit a flaming iceberg!"

Women and Children First

𝓘 never saw the iceberg, nor did any of us stokers, but we soon met one of the crew who was there when the ship struck, and who had seen it all. He said the iceberg was at least a hundred feet high, looming above the ship, and not white like icebergs are supposed to be, but dark, almost black. But it had been a glancing blow, he said, no cause for alarm, no need for panic. And no one was panicking. No one was rushing anywhere. By now more and more passengers were beginning to appear on deck, to find out what was happening, just as we had. I saw a couple strolling by arm in arm. They looked completely unconcerned, as if they were simply taking the air. Even after the collision, like everyone on board, they clearly still accepted, as I did, the absolute assumption – and one that had after all been confirmed to me in person of course by Captain Smith himself – that the *Titanic* was unsinkable, that everything would be all right.

It was when the ship began to list, and this happened quite soon, that the first doubts began to creep in. But only when I saw men and women gathering in numbers on deck, and putting on their life-preservers, did I truly begin to understand the dreadful danger we were now in, and only then did I think of Lizziebeth and Kaspar in their stateroom on deck C. It took me a while to locate the right corridor, and when I did I had some difficulty in finding my way to number 52. There was no time to stand on ceremony. I hammered on the door, yelling for them. A moment or two later Mr Stanton was standing there, in front of me, his face grey with anxiety. He was fully dressed, with his life-preserver already on, as were the rest of the family.

They looked at me as if I'd come from another planet. I just blurted it out. "I stowed away." That was all I said by way of explanation. There wasn't time for any more, and now it didn't matter anyway.

"Are we sinking?" Mrs Stanton asked me. She was quite calm and controlled.

"I don't know," I said. "I don't think so. But I think we should get out on deck."

Mrs Stanton was picking up her bag.

"We must take nothing with us, my dear." Mr Stanton

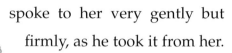

spoke to her very gently but firmly, as he took it from her. "But all my precious things, my mother's necklace, my photographs," she cried.

"You and Lizziebeth are all that's precious," he said quietly. He turned to me. "Johnny, you will take care of Lizziebeth." Lizziebeth's hand had crept into mine. It was cold. She looked up at me, her eyes full of bewilderment. She seemed still only half awake. It was only as we were leaving the cabin that she seemed to begin to comprehend what was going on. She grabbed her father's arm suddenly. "Papa, what about Kaspar? We can't leave Kaspar."

"We leave everything behind, Lizziebeth, and I mean everything." Mr Stanton spoke very firmly to her. "Now follow me and stay close." Staying close was not easy because the corridors and gangways were full of people, and many of them were carrying or dragging heavy bags. Lizziebeth kept saying it again and again, to me now, "What about Kaspar? We can't leave him Johnny, we can't. Please. All those people, they've got bags, they're carrying things. Please." She was trying to tug me back all the time, but I knew there was nothing I could say to comfort her. I had to ignore her and keep going.

As we got up on to the Boat Deck and out into the cold air I realised that the ship was listing noticeably more severely than before. I saw dozens of post bags being piled up on deck, and abandoned luggage everywhere. Boats were being lowered away, and the band was playing. Everywhere people were gathered in small groups, huddling together against the cold, some with blankets round their shoulders A few were praying aloud, but most stood in silence, waiting patiently.

I recognised Mr Lightoller, the officer we'd seen in the Captain's cabin, going about the deck, organising, spreading calm as he went, and explaining to everyone that it would be women and children first, that when all the women and children were safely away in the lifeboats, then the men could leave. When he turned to Mrs Stanton and told her it was her turn to get into one of the boats, she clung to her husband and refused.

"I won't leave my family," she said. "We belong together, and if it's God's will, then we will die together."

Mr Stanton took her gently by the shoulders and, looking deep into her eyes, he spoke to her very softly, almost in a whisper. "You will take Lizziebeth, my dear, and you will do as the officer says, and go to the boat. Johnny Trott and I will come after you, I promise you. Go, my dear. Go now."

At that moment Lizziebeth broke free of my hand and ran for it. I knew straight away that she was going back for Kaspar. I went after her at once, and caught her at the top of the gangway. She struggled against me, but I held her tight. "I can't leave him!" she cried. "I can't! I won't!"

"Lizziebeth," I said. "Listen to me. I must take you to the boat. It'll be gone soon. You have to go with your mother. You have to save yourself. Leave Kaspar to me. I'll find him. I'll save him."

She looked up at me, her eyes full of sudden hope. "You promise me?"

"I promise," I told her.

"And you, Johnny, what will happen to you?"

"I'll be all right, there's plenty of boats," I said.

When we got back to the railings, the lifeboat was nearly full and

almost ready to launch, but
I could see the crew were
having the greatest difficulty
in lowering it. With the
help of Mr Stanton
and a sailor we
helped Lizziebeth
and her mother
into the boat.

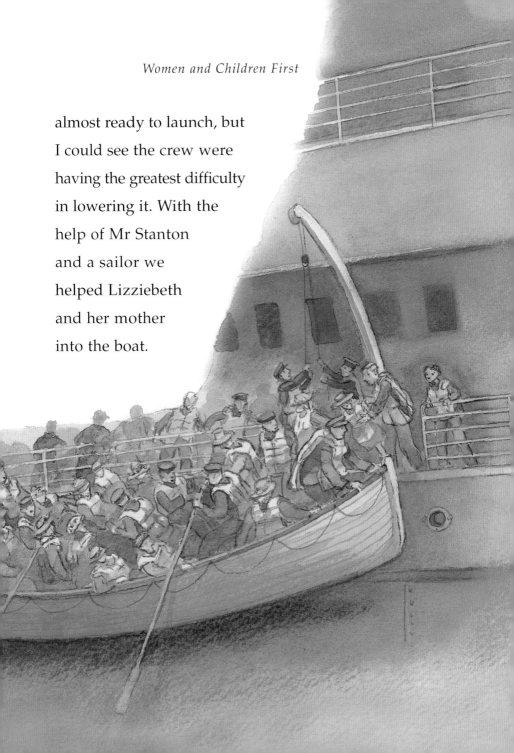

But still the boat could not be lowered. One of the crew was slicing away at the rope with his knife, cursing as he did so, and cursing even louder when he dropped his knife into the sea below. There were several lifeboats in the water already and rowing away from the *Titanic*. I glanced towards the stern and saw it was a great deal higher than it had been before. I could feel the great ship settling ever lower into the sea.

I caught Lizziebeth's eye then. She was willing me to do it, and to do it now. I knew that if I left it any longer it may well be too late. I would show her there and then that I meant to keep my promise if I could. I turned to Mr Stanton beside me. "I'm going for Kaspar," I said. "I shan't be long." He shouted after me to come back, but I ignored him.

By now the decks were crowded with men, all of them corralled by the crew who had made a human cordon to keep them back as the last of the women and children were being helped into the boats. But there was no pushing, no shoving. I saw among them dozens of my fellow stokers, most of them black with coal dust, and all unnaturally quiet. As I pushed my way through them to get back down below, one of them called out to me. "You should be in one of they boats, Johnny lad. You're only a slip of a boy. You're young enough. You've got the right."

The gangway was packed with passengers trying to make their way up on deck, some of the older and more infirm still in their nightgowns. One of the sailors who was trying to help them tried to stop me going down. "You can't go. There's water coming in everywhere down there, the whole ship's flooding fast." I dodged past him. "Idiot!" he yelled after me. "You blithering idiot! You go down there and you won't come back up again!" I ran on.

After losing my way in the warren of corridors,

I reached the right corridor on deck C and I knew then that the sailor had been right. The sea-water was ankle deep, and rising all the time. And once I opened the door to number 52, I saw the carpets were already under water. I looked around me frantically for Kaspar, but couldn't see him anywhere, not at first. It was Kaspar himself who told me where he was, yowling at me from the top of the wardrobe. I looked around for the picnic basket to carry him in, but couldn't find it. I reached up and took him off the wardrobe, and held him tight; but then, as I went out, I had the presence of mind to snatch a blanket off the nearest bed. All the way back along the corridor, I was wrapping Kasper up in the blanket, not against the cold, but to stop him clawing at me, for I knew that even if he wasn't frightened now, he very soon would be.

But as I ran back down the corridor I was beginning to realise that the blanket had another use, and a much more essential one too. If no luggage was being allowed in the boats, I reasoned, then they would hardly accept a cat. This was why, by the time I got back up on deck again, Kaspar was well hidden deep inside the blanket. And now he was beginning to yowl.

"None of your fuss, please Kaspar," I whispered to him. "Quiet now, and stay quiet. Your life could depend on it."

I pushed my way through the stokers, ducked under the cordon of crewmen, and saw to my great relief that the lifeboat was still hanging there. But then I found my way suddenly blocked by an officer in a peaked cap, who grabbed me by the shoulder. "No you don't, lad. No men allowed in the boats until all the women and children are loaded," he said. "I can't let you on. I can't let you pass."

"He's not a man," someone shouted from behind me. "He's only a kid, can't you see?" All around me the stokers were suddenly clamouring at him to let me through, and they began pushing angrily against the ring of sailors desperately trying to hold them back. I could see the officer was taken by surprise at the sudden rage of the crowd, and that he was hesitating.

I saw my chance. "I'm not going on the boat," I told him. "I just went to fetch a blanket. It's for a child, a friend of mine. She'll freeze to death out there without it." I still don't think he'd have let me through if Mr Stanton hadn't come up at that moment and vouched for me.

"It's all right. He's my son," he said to the officer, "and the blanket's for his sister." I was through. With Mr Stanton holding me fast round the waist I leaned across and handed the blanket, and the miraculously silent Kaspar, into Mrs Stanton's outstretched arms.

"Be careful," I told her as meaningfully as I could. She knew as she was taking it from me that Kaspar was inside the blanket. She hugged it to her and sat down again in the boat. I could see from the way Lizziebeth was smiling up at me that she knew it too.

Distress rockets were fired up into the sky, lighting the ocean all around us, lighting too the scattering of little white boats out on the open sea, each of them crammed with women and children.

I remember thinking how extraordinarily beautiful it all was, and wondering how something as terrible as this could be so beautiful. On board behind us the band played on, as Lizziebeth's boat was finally lowered into the water. Mr Stanton and I stood side by side and watched from the railings as it was rowed slowly away. "That was a fine and noble thing you did, Johnny," he said, putting his hand on my shoulder. "God will guard them, I know it. And for us there'll be a boat along soon enough to take us off. Mr Lightoller says they've seen the lights of a ship not five miles away. The *Carpathia*. She'll be on her way. They'll see these rockets for sure. They'll be alongside soon enough. Meanwhile, I think we should help with the women and children, don't you?" That was how we busied ourselves for the next hour or so, passing the women and the children into the boats.

I marvel now when I think of it, at the courage I witnessed around me that night. I saw one American lady waiting to get into a boat with her elderly sister, but she was told there was no room. She didn't object or protest in anyway, but merely stepped back and said: "Never mind. I will get on a later boat." I never saw her again. I saw no man ever try to push his way to the boats. To a man they accepted that it was perfectly right and proper for women and children to go first. I heard later that some men on the starboard side of the ship had tried to rush one of the lifeboats, and that shots had to be fired over their heads to drive them back. But I never saw it with my own eyes.

There were many heroes that night, but if there was one I remember best it was Mr Lightoller. He was everywhere, quietly ensuring the safe loading and launching of the boats, and picking out the seamen to row each one. I can hear his voice even now echoing in my head. "Lower away there. Lower away. Are there any more women? Are there any more women?" And one of the waiting men answered him back, I remember.

"No more women, Officer. There's plenty of men though, but I don't see plenty of boats."

It was something every one of us now had come to realise, that there were hardly any boats left to take the rest of us off, and that many of the lifeboats that remained could not now be launched because of the severe list of the ship. When I saw the sea-water come washing over the bow, and rushing down the deck towards us, I knew that our chances of survival were fading fast. Like so many others, I scanned the horizon desperately for the lights of the *Carpathia*. We were all aware by now that she was the only ship close enough to come to our rescue. But there were no lights to be seen.

The *Titanic* was sinking fast, and we knew now we were going down with her. With every minute that passed now the list to port was telling us the end was near. The deck was at such an angle that it was well-nigh impossible to keep our footing. We heard Mr Lightoller's voice ringing out. "All passengers to the starboard side."

So that's where Mr Stanton and I went, slipping and sliding, clutching at each other for support, until we reached the rail on the starboard side and clung on. Here we looked out at the sea, and waited silently for our end. There was nothing more to be done. "I should like to say," Mr Stanton said, his hand resting on my shoulder, "that if I am to die tonight and I cannot die with my family, then I'd rather die in your company than any other. You're a fine young man, Johnny Trott."

"Will the sea be cold?" I asked him.

"I fear so," he replied, "but don't worry, that's all to the good. It will all be over very quickly for us both."

"Good Luck and God Bless You"

It was our blessed good fortune that Mr Stanton and I were there on the Boat Deck at the time the last boat was being lowered. It was not one of the large wooden lifeboats – they were all gone by now – but one of the boats with canvas sides, some twenty or more feet long, with a rounded hull. This one was stored below a funnel and there were some men trying to manhandle it down on to the deck, a couple of crew among them. One of them was shouting at us: "This is the only boat left, this is our only chance. We need more hands here!" Wading though water that was waist-high by now, Mr Stanton and I and a dozen other men did all we could to help them heave the boat up and over the rail. All of us knew this was our last hope. How we strained and struggled to launch that lifeboat, but it was too heavy and too cumbersome for us. There weren't enough of us, and we were very soon exhausted by our efforts. We couldn't do it. The *Titanic* was groaning and gasping all about us. She was going down at the bow, fast.

I looked up to see a great wave come rolling along the decks towards us, a lucky wave as it turned out. It swept the lifeboat overboard and we went with it. The shock of the icy sea drove all the breath from my body and left me gasping for breath.

I remember trying to swim frantically away from the ship, and then looking back and seeing one of the huge funnels breaking away and falling down on top of me, toppling like a giant tree. As it hit the water I felt myself sucked under and swirled away downwards into a whirlpool of such power I was sure it would take me to the bottom with the ship. All I could do was to keep my mouth pursed, tight shut, and my eyes open.

Suddenly I saw Mr Stanton above me, his feet caught in a rope. He was kicking and struggling to break free. Then, miraculously, I was released from the whirlpool, and found I could swim up towards him. I managed to free him from the rope, and together we swam hard for the surface, for the light. How deep we were by now I had no idea. All I knew was that I had to swim with all my strength, and not to breathe, not to open my mouth. What I learned that night was what every drowning man learns before he dies, that in the end he has to open his mouth and try to breathe. That is how he drowns. When at last I had to take a breath the sea rushed in and choked me, but at that very moment I broke the surface, spluttering, coughing the water out of my lungs. Mr Stanton was in the water nearby, calling for me. We saw the upturned lifeboat nearby, and swam towards it. There were bodies floating in the water, hundreds of them. The cold was cramping my legs, sapping what little strength I still had. If I didn't reach the boat, if I didn't get out of the water and soon, I would be as lifeless as those bodies all around me. I swam for my life.

There were other survivors clambering on to it

when we got there, and I couldn't see how there'd be room for us as well. But helping hands hauled us both up out of the sea and we joined them there, half standing, half lying back against the upturned hull of the lifeboat, and clinging to one another for dear life. Only then did I really begin to take in the horrors of the tragedy I had been living through. The shrieks and cries of the drowning were all around me. I caught my last sight of the great *Titanic*, her stern almost vertical, slipping into the sea. When she was gone we were left only with the debris of this dreadful disaster strewn all around the ocean, and those terrible cries that went on and on. And there were swimmers in the sea all around us, every one of them, it seemed, heading our way. Very soon we were swamped with them and we were turning them away, yelling at any others who came near that there was no room. And that was true, horribly true.

The buoyancy of our boat was already under threat. We were low in the water as it was, and all of us would be lost if we took on any more. What I have never forgotten is that even in their desperate plight many of those swimmers seemed to understand the situation perfectly, and accept it. One of them – and I recognised him as one of the stokers I'd worked alongside – said to us, his voice shaking with cold: "All right then, lads, good luck and God bless you." And with that he swam off in among the bodies, and the chairs and the crates, and disappeared.

I never saw him again.

I will carry to the grave the guilt of what we did to that man and to so many others. Like so many survivors I have lived through that night out on the open ocean in my dreams, again and again. Mr Stanton and I did not talk much, each of us too busy with our own doubts and dreads, too busy just surviving. But side by side we endured together. I know that for me it was memories that kept me going. I think I relived most of my life that night: Harry the cockroach in his matchbox, the Countess Kandinsky sweeping into the Savoy in her ostrich feather hat, taking her bows at the opera that night, Kaspar curled up on her piano as she sang, Lizziebeth beaming up at me as she fed him his liver, Lizziebeth on the roof of the Savoy, Lizziebeth and her mother in the lifeboat with Kaspar hidden in his blanket.

Around us the ocean was silent and empty now. There were no more cries for help, no more last messages to mother, no more appeals to God. We looked, and we never stopped looking, for the lights of a ship on the horizon that might bring us some hope of rescue. Our lifeboat had floated away from all the others by now and from all the wreckage that had littered the ocean. We were quite alone and quite helpless. From time to time one of our number – there were about thirty of us, I think – said the Lord's Prayer, but for the most part we were silent.

The growing fear for all of us as the night passed was the sea itself. At the time the ship went down the ocean was completely calm, just as it had been ever since we left Southampton. But now all of us could feel that a swell was building, and we all knew that if the waves worsened our fragile craft would be bound to sink beneath us. Sleep too was a danger. Already one of the older passengers had simply fallen asleep and slipped into the sea. He went down without a struggle. I saw him go, and I knew then that very soon I would be going the same way. I wasn't afraid of dying, not any more. I just wanted to get it over with. Often I felt coming over me an irresistible wish to surrender myself to sleep, only for Mr Stanton to shake me back to my senses.

It was Mr Stanton too who first saw the lights of

the *Carpathia*. His cracked voice shouted it out to the rest of us. Some did not believe it at first because the rise and fall of the swell intermittently hid the lights from us. But soon they were quite unmistakable. A great joy surged through every one of us, giving us new strength and new determination. Not that any of us cheered, but when we looked at each other now we could manage a smile. We knew we had a chance to survive. Those lights of hope, lights of life, for that's what they were for us, drove away the darkness of our despair, and the agony of the cold too. Mr Stanton's arm came round my shoulder. I knew he must be hoping what I was hoping for, that his wife, and his daughter, and Kaspar might be there on the *Carpathia*, and safe.

We did not know it at the time, but we were the last survivors to be picked up by the *Carpathia*. I went up the rope ladder ahead of Mr Stanton.

My legs were so weak that I wondered often as I climbed whether I could make it or not. I could see that my hands were gripping the ladder, but I couldn't feel them. It wasn't strength that got me up that ladder, it was nothing but the will to live. Then with Mr Stanton and all the others from the lifeboat we were all taken below into the warm, given dry clothes and swathed in blankets. We sat there drinking warm, sweet tea. It has been my favourite drink ever since.

There was chaos on board. It was no one's fault. The crew of the *Carpathia* were doing their best, but they were overwhelmed, they were busy just coping as best they could. Whoever we asked, no one seemed to have any definite news of anyone. Lists of survivors were being compiled, we were told.

Mr Stanton asked the sailors repeatedly for news of his family, but there was no one who recognised their description. Every one of us on that ship was looking for someone. Many sat silent, already knowing the worst, lost in grief. Joyous reunions were few and far between. Fearful and hopeful, we went looking for Lizziebeth and Mrs Stanton and Kaspar. We searched the ship from bow to stern. They were nowhere to be found. We found bodies lying on the deck, though, wrapped in blankets. We checked these too. I came across one little girl, about the same age as Lizziebeth, and was sure it was her at first, but it was not.

We looked everywhere we could think of, asked again and again the same question. The last lingering hope left to us was that they might still be out there at sea in their lifeboat. The two of us went to the ship's rail. But all the lifeboats we saw floating around the ship were already empty. We scanned the sea all around, searched the horizon. There was nothing. At that moment of utter despair we heard a yowling from behind us. We turned. They were there, all three of them, shrouded in blankets, only their faces showing. It was a strange and wonderful reunion for all of us. We stood there on the deck for many long minutes, our arms around one another. It was during those moments I really felt for the first time that I had in some way become one of them, one of the family.

Crowded in a cabin below with other survivors, we slept and told our stories and slept again. Lizziebeth and her mother owed their survival, they told us, to a small Japanese man who spoke no English and a brave French lady who fortunately spoke both Japanese and English, so could translate. Through her, the Japanese man made it quite clear to everyone that they should do what he was doing and row. If they rowed they would keep warm, he said, and keeping warm could save their lives. So that's what they did, taking it in turns all night long. Even Lizziebeth rowed. She sat on the French lady's lap and rowed. Because of that wonderful man's example, Mrs Stanton said, not one of them had died of the cold in that lifeboat. His example and his cheerfulness had kept their spirits up all through the longest, coldest night of their lives, and when they reached the *Carpathia*, he was the last out of the lifeboat.

I knew even as she was telling us that it had to be Little Mitch. I went searching for him at once, and found him after a while on his own, looking out over the railings at the empty sea. We greeted each other as old friends, which of course after all we had lived through, we most certainly were. I was up on deck with Little Mitch a few days later, as the *Carpathia* steamed slowly in to New York Harbour. That was when we first set eyes on the Statue of Liberty. He turned to me with a big grin on his face, and said just one word: "America!"

A New Life

That was how Kaspar and I came to America, as stowaways, as survivors from the *Titanic*. When we docked in New York we came down the gangplank of the *Carpathia* together, the Stanton family and Kaspar and me. Mr Stanton had "a discussion", as he called it, with the immigration authorities, and as a consequence of this I was allowed to go and stay

with them in their house in Greenwich Village.
From the very start I was treated as if I was one of
them. I was told I should never again call them Mr
and Mrs Stanton, no more "Sir" or "Madam". It
would be Robert and Ann from now on. I found this
very difficult at first – old habits die hard – but it
became ever more natural as the weeks passed.

But then Lizziebeth fell sick, very sick. The
terrible cold of that night on the ocean had reached
her lungs, and she'd caught pneumonia. The doctor
came often to begin with, a taciturn man who did
little to relieve our anxiety. Kaspar stayed with her
all through her illness, scarcely ever leaving her bed.
All the rest of us would take it in turns to sit with
her. Then one morning I came in and she was sitting
up in bed, with Kaspar on her lap, and smiling at
me. She was her sunny self again. But for some time
afterwards she still had to stay in her room and rest,
which she didn't care for at all, not one bit.

Lizziebeth claimed that it *had* to be Kaspar who had brought luck to all of us. Because of Kaspar, she said, they had survived the night in the boat, and because of Kaspar she had recovered from her pneumonia.

I had a big argument with her about that. Much as I loved Kaspar, I never much believed in superstitions. You might as well say, I told her, that it was Kaspar who had brought us bad luck in the first place, the worst luck, that maybe it was because Kaspar was on board that the *Titanic* had sunk in the first place. "Nonsense," Lizziebeth retorted. "It was an iceberg, not Kaspar, that sank the *Titanic*!" I think I discovered then, if I hadn't before, that I could never have an argument with Lizziebeth and expect to win, that one way or another she would always have the last word.

During Lizziebeth's convalescence, when she still wasn't allowed out of the house, I got to know Robert and Ann a great deal better. It took a while for me to feel completely at ease with them when we were alone, and I think they sensed it. They took it upon themselves to give me a good time, to show me New York. We went up the Empire State Building, visited the Statue of Liberty, and the zoo – all of which made Lizziebeth very jealous – and once we went collecting horseshoe crab shells on a beach on Long Island. Best of all, I learned to ride with Ann in Central Park. She took me riding almost every day. I hadn't been on a horse before, so I had a lot to learn, but Ann was full of encouragement. "You ride so well, Johnny," she told me once, "as if you'd been born in the saddle. I'm very proud of you." The truth is that I loved being with them whatever we were doing. I felt as if I was a son for the first time. Having a mother and father of my own was better than I had ever imagined it could be. I was having the time of my life.

In the evenings I'd be up in Lizziebeth's room, playing with Kaspar if he was awake, and learning how to play chess with Lizziebeth when he wasn't. I liked chess, although I never managed to win a single game against her. As for Kaspar, he had the run of the place as I did, and very soon had occupied the piano in the drawing room and made it his own. Everyone in the house, Lizziebeth's governess, the servants too, all simply adored him.

Like me, he couldn't have been happier. Only one cloud hung over me, the knowledge that sooner or later all these golden days would have to end, and I'd have to leave. How I dreaded that day.

One evening, some months afterwards, I was called down into the drawing room to find the family all lined up in front of the fireplace. Lizziebeth was in her dressing gown. Kaspar was sitting on the piano watching me, his tail swishing. Lizziebeth was looking at me conspiratorially – clearly she knew something I didn't. Her mother and father on the other hand were looking very serious and stiff, rather as they had been when I'd first seen them that time back in their rooms at the Savoy Hotel. This is it, I thought, this is when they tell me my time's up, that I have to go back to London, to my job as a bell-boy in the Savoy.

Robert cleared his throat. He was going to make some kind of a speech. I prepared myself for the worst. "Johnny, the three of us have come to a decision," he began. "You know how much we have enjoyed having you with us here as our guest. Lizziebeth has told us of your circumstances back home in England, that you have no family as such to go back to…" He hesitated, and that was when Ann spoke up.

"I guess what we're trying to say, Johnny, is that after all that has happened, and knowing you now as well as we do, and what a fine young man you are, we would very much like you to consider not returning to London, but instead staying here and making your home with us in New York. We'd be really proud to have you live here as one of the family, if you'd like it that is. What do you say?"

I remember Kaspar and Lizziebeth both looking up at me, waiting for me to say something. It took me a while – not to make up my mind – I did that instantly, but to get over my surprise and find my voice.

"Oh come on, Johnny Trott, say yes, please," Lizziebeth cried.

"OK," I replied – it was a new expression I'd picked up in New York. I was so overwhelmed that it was all I could bring myself to say. But it was enough. Everyone hugged me then, and we all cried a little, except Kaspar who had sprung up on the piano, and was busy washing himself.

So, by the greatest of good fortune, I acquired a new life, a new home, and a new country. They sent me back to school, which at first I didn't care for. I thought I'd finished with all that – I'd never been much good at books and reading and all that. But Robert read stories to us all in the evenings, and through him I came to like books a lot better than I had. Gradually school became much easier, and sometimes even enjoyable. They teased me a bit at first on account of my London cockney accent, and so to start with I felt a bit alone. But someone put it about that I was a survivor from the *Titanic*, and after that I had all the friends I could handle. We spent long summers in Maine, sailing up there on the *Abe Lincoln*. Lizziebeth and I went walking in the woods and fishing, and everywhere we went Kaspar came with us. They were great days, days I shall remember all my life.

I was to have gone off to college, to William and Mary in Virginia, where Robert himself had once been a student. I never got there. In Europe the First World War was raging, and my old country was fighting for her life. So when in 1917 America sent troops over to fight in France, I went with them. And who did I find marching alongside me up to the front? Little Mitch. We just picked up where we'd left off all those years before on the *Titanic*, on the *Carpathia*, and were best friends from then on.

While I was at the front I'd get letters every week from Lizziebeth, who was away at boarding school by now. I'd look forward to every one of them because I could hear her voice in her writing, see her face as I was reading her words, and that cheered me more than I can say, when all around me in France I saw nothing but horror and death. And with her letters Lizziebeth would sometimes send me little sketches, and once a beautiful drawing of Kaspar sitting there looking at me, willing me to come home it seemed. I kept it with me in my tunic pocket, along with a photograph of her and me by the sea-shore in Maine. Lizziebeth always said afterwards, when the war was over, that it must have been the drawing of Kaspar that had kept me safe and brought me home. I'm not sure she was right about that, but she insisted on having it framed and put up in pride of place in the front hall. When no one's looking, I do reach out and touch it sometimes. So I suppose that I must be just a little superstitious. But I'm not admitting that to her.

Right after the war Mitch came to work with me

in Robert's publishing business – he had become quite a family friend by now. We worked together in the packing room in the basement – Robert said we had to learn the business from the bottom upwards. So we did, literally. For me, books became a part of my life. I didn't just pack them, I read them voraciously, and very soon began to write stories of my own. And while I was writing, Lizziebeth would be up in her attic studio, drawing or painting or sculpting, animals mostly. On our holidays in Maine we wouldn't climb trees any more, or go diving off the quay, she'd sit on the rocks by the seashore with her sketchbook out, and I'd scribble away nearby, and Kaspar would wander between us to remind us he was there. We would often talk of the old days in London, of Mr Freddie and Skullface, and the great roof rescue. And more than once she said what fun it would be to go back to visit. But I didn't think she was serious.

Then just before her seventeenth birthday she

announced to us that she was too old now to be given birthday presents. Instead she was going to give us something, providing, she added, that we didn't mind giving it away. None of us knew quite what to make of this, until she took us out into the front hall. And there it was. Sitting on the table, below the famous sketch she had sent out to me in France during the war, was a magnificent sculpture of Kaspar, his neck arched, his tail curled around him. "I carved it out of ash wood," she said, "and then I painted it jet black. And do you know

what I want? I want to take it back to London, and give it to the hotel where we stayed, where I first saw Kaspar and Johnny. I want it to be there for ever. It's where Kaspar belongs. Kaspar could come too. He may be old, but he's fit as a fiddle. Well?" she said, beaming brightly at us. "When do we go?"

We went six months later, and Little Mitch came with us too. We wanted him to come, to show him where it had all happened, where the whole story had begun, a story he was part of, that had changed all our lives for ever. I won't pretend that any of us much enjoyed the crossing of the Atlantic. There were too many terrible memories, but we kept them to ourselves, and never once mentioned the *Titanic*. In fact we had hardly ever mentioned the *Titanic* in all these years. It was what bound us inseparably, and what distanced us from others who had not been there, but we had rarely spoken of it among ourselves. All together again on the wide Atlantic, we faced our fears, and took strength from one another's silence.

Mr Freddie was there to greet us at the front door of the Savoy, and when we went inside, the staff were waiting to welcome us. Kaspar yowled from his basket as they all clapped us in. So I took him out to show everyone. He loved all the attention, and to tell the truth, so did I. Mary O'Connell was still there, head housekeeper now, instead of Skullface. She gave Ann a huge bunch of red roses, and cried on my shoulder as she hugged me. As for the bell-boy who took us up in the lift, he was a cockney lad, just like me, wearing the same uniform, with his cap worn at the same jaunty angle. He showed us into the Countess Kandinsky's old rooms, with windows looking out over the Thames down towards the Houses of Parliament. Kaspar made himself at home at once, resuming his place on the piano and proceeding to washing himself vigorously. He was as happy as I'd ever seen him.

He slept on the window ledge in the sun all the rest of that day. He'd been doing a lot of sleeping lately.

We had an unveiling ceremony outside the American Bar the next morning, and much to Lizziebeth's delight, everyone seemed to like the sculpture as much as they loved Kaspar himself. He was there at the ceremony, but wandered off during the speeches. I watched him go, waving his tail as he went. It was the last I ever saw of him. He just disappeared. Everyone searched the hotel, over and over again, from the basement to the attic corridor. He was nowhere to be found.

It's well enough known that old cats go off to die when they're good and ready. I think, and Lizziebeth thinks, that's what he must have done. We were sad, of course we were. He was the cat that had brought us together, had survived with us, and he was gone. But in a way, as I told Lizziebeth, trying to comfort her, he is not gone. He's sitting there proudly outside the American Bar. You can go and see him for yourself, if you like. He's still there, looking very pleased with himself, and so he should be. After all, he is Prince Kaspar Kandinsky, Prince of Cats, a Muscovite, a Londoner and a New Yorker, and as far as anyone knows, the only cat to survive the sinking of the *Titanic*.

And then...

...only a year or so after our visit to London, we received a letter from Mr Freddie.

Dear Johnny and Lizziebeth,

I'm writing to tell you of a strange happening. Several guests at the hotel have reported sighting a black cat wandering the corridors late at night. I took no notice at first, but it has happened time and again, and I thought you ought to know. And just yesterday, a lady staying in your rooms, the Countess Kandinsky's rooms, reported seeing a reflection in the mirror of a grand lady in an ostrich-feathered hat, carrying a black cat in her arms. When she was offered the opportunity to be moved to another room, she said she'd rather stay, that they were kindly ghosts, like good companions. Mary and the others send love. Come and see us again one day, before too long.

Yours, Freddie

Postscript

I'm a story detective. I hunt down clues because I need evidence to write my stories. So what was the evidence behind the writing of Kaspar?

A year ago I was asked to be Writer-in-Residence at the Savoy Hotel in London. This involved putting on some literary events and staying for three months at the Savoy. My wife Clare and I had a bed the size of Ireland, and breakfast every morning looking out over the Thames. Everyone in the hotel was very kind. We were treated like royalty – which was great!

Then one day, in the corridor next to the American Bar, I met Kaspar, the Savoy Cat. He was sitting there in a glass showcase – a sculpture of a huge black cat – very elegant, very superior. I made enquiries, as detectives do, and found out why he was there.

One day, almost a hundred years ago, thirteen men sat down to a dinner party at the Savoy. One of them scoffed loudly at the suggestion that thirteen might be an unlucky number, said it was so much tosh. Only a few weeks later, he was shot down in his office in Johannesburg, South Africa. Thereafter The Savoy decided that they would never again allow thirteen people to sit down together for dinner. They would always have a fourteenth chair, and sitting on the fourteenth chair, there would be a specially carved sculpture of a lucky black cat. He was known as Kaspar.

My first clue.

My second clue: I came down to breakfast one morning, and was walking down the red carpeted stairs into the River Restaurant, when I looked up and had a sudden sense of déjà vu. The whole decor and atmosphere reminded me of pictures I'd seen of the restaurant on the Titanic. I knew then my story would be about a cat called Kaspar, who would live at the Savoy and become the only cat to survive the sinking of the Titanic.

But it was the people who lived and worked at the Savoy who gave me my last and my most vital clue. I discovered that they came from every corner of the globe. And I soon discovered also that their lives were very different from the lives of the guests they looked after. It would have been very much like this, I thought, in 1912, at the time the Titanic went down.

My evidence was complete. A little dreamtime, to make some sense of all the clues, and I could begin my story, about how Kaspar was brought to the Savoy by a very famous diva – an opera singer, a Countess from Russia... You know the rest by now, unless you've read this postscript first – I'll be very cross with you if you have!

MICHAEL MORPURGO